THE LOST MINE

It was an unlikely partnership — Thad Lynch, an upright Union officer, and a murderous Confederate, the burly Sergeant Jack. What united them was an ancient map and its clues to finding the fabulous gold of the Lost Mine of the Superstitions. Rumour had it that whoever went looking for it was doomed to die, or to return crazy in the head. Could Lynch and Jack beat the jinx? Could they fight off Black Wolf? Many bullets and arrows would fly before these questions could be answered.

JOHN DYSON

THE LOST MINE

Complete and Unabridged

LINFORD
Leicester

First published in Great Britain in 2003 by
Robert Hale Limited
London

First Linford Edition
published 2005
by arrangement with
Robert Hale Limited
London

British Library CIP Data

Dyson, John, *1943* –
The lost mine.—Large print ed.—
Linford western library
1. Western stories
2. Large type books
I. Title
823.9'14 [F]

ISBN 1–84395–606–3

Published by
F. A. Thorpe (Publishing)
Anstey, Leicestershire

Set by Words & Graphics Ltd.
Anstey, Leicestershire
Printed and bound in Great Britain by
T. J. International Ltd., Padstow, Cornwall

This book is printed on acid-free paper

To the memory of my favourite
F.A.N.Y. Bunty Hancock, an
unsung heroine of WWII who
started me writing westerns forty
books ago. We had great fun along
the way. Alas, no more.

1

Towering red cliffs, a thousand feet high, enclosed the dusty waste of Hell Canyon. Hidden among the rocks and slurry at the foot of the cliffs, twenty men sat on their mustangs, ready-cocked revolvers in their hands, eagerly watching an ornate coach, drawn by six horses, which lumbered along the base of the canyon in the dark shadows cast by the mesas. They were a rough-looking bunch, greasy hats pulled low over their bearded faces, in dusty range-clothes, tense as hawks, ready to swoop into action.

'They got two outriders'. A part-Paiute Indian, known as Black Wolf, pointed to two Mexicans in wide-brimmed sombreros who rode slightly ahead of the coach. 'They must be carryin' something valuable.'

'There's the driver, the shotgun,

maybe a couple more men inside. That only makes six. We can take 'em.'

The speaker was a swarthy, black-bearded individual in a curly-brimmed top hat that had seen better days, and a worn, caped greatcoat. The ruddiness of his fleshy nose revealed a liking for liquor. But what distinguished him was a two-pronged iron contraption, like a pair of pincers, attached to his shorn right forearm. It did not prevent him from raising a long-barrelled Henry rifle. He squinted along the sights as he fingered the trigger with his left forefinger.

'I can take 'em out,' he growled.

'Hold your horses!' Black Wolf barked out. He appeared to be in command. 'Let's wait 'til they git real close. We got the advantage of surprise.'

The 'breed was attired Western fashion, in red blanket-cloth shirt, fringed shotgun chaps, a gun belt around his waist, and high-crowned black hat. But beaded moccasins, his long, dark hair, and a bow with a quiver

2

of arrows slung across his back, revealed his mixed blood. From one aspect he appeared a lean, prow-nosed, handsome man, but when he turned his head it showed that half his face had been hideously ruined by the swipe of a grizzly's claw. A black patch covered the empty eye-socket.

'Look at that gilded coach,' he said. 'That don't belong to anybody. My guess is it's some rich *haciendado*. This could be our lucky day, boys.'

'Yeah.' His companion, known as Sergeant Jack, growled. 'Remember, don't let any git away. Leave no witnesses, thass my motto. That way none of us gits strung up.'

Inside the heavy, old-fashioned coach there was indeed, a silver-haired *haciendado*, Don Miguel Bernardino Pico, his wife, Doña Esmeralda, holding her six-month-old baby, and her maid, Julia. But Don Pico had fallen on hard times and carried very little gold coin with him, just sufficient to cover their journey up from Sonora to Tucson.

3

There he planned to auction an ancient parchment map which had been held by his family for centuries. His hopes were that it would raise a large amount of ready cash. He carried it not in their trunks of luggage but wrapped in stout linen and attached to his right thigh beneath his pearl-grey summer suit.

'How much further?' Doña Esmeralda wore a flowing white pleated summer-dress, pinned at the throat by a gold-and-and-ruby brooch. She peered wearily and warily out of the leather dust-shutter at the harsh cliffside. At least they had been assured that the Apache were pacified and were no threat to their safety. 'The baby is very fretful. Will you take her, Julia?'

'Not much further to the way station.' Don Pico tried to reassure her, although they would need to travel all day. 'We will be in Tucson in two more days.'

'Oh, Lord!' Esmeralda groaned. 'Why did we ever set out on this foolish journey?'

'Needs must.' Don Miguel's eyes widened with alarm as he heard a rifle shot crack out and as he peered from the shutter on his side of the coach, saw his foreman *charro*, Jose, throw up his arms and go spinning from his horse into the dust.

'Oh, Jesus!' he cried, crossing himself. He heard a clatter of revolver shots and a gang of riders poured down from the rocks charging towards them. He stared at his wife and child with an expression of horror, aware that these might be their last moments on earth. Then he reached for his revolver and, poking it through the shutter began firing at the desperadoes, now fast bearing down upon them.

'Keep you heads down,' he yelled in Spanish as a bullet ripped past him to embed in the seat's upholstery. At risk to his life he leaned out of the window and shouted to the coachman: 'For God's sake, Jorge, keep going!'

As he spoke Jorge tumbled from the box and was left in a heap behind them.

The coach began to slow. The guard loosed both barrels of his shotgun at the marauders, but he, too, received the same rough treatment and slumped dead on the box. The lone *charro* put up a spirited resistance. He was no match for a band of murderous ex-Confederates.

He was shot from the saddle and left lying in the dust.

The coach slowed to a halt, hauled in by one of the *bandidos*. Don Miguel stared at his wife and child. He had two bullets left. Would it be better to end their sufferings quickly? He shook his head and sighed.

'Maybe they only intend to rob us.'

In response to a shouted command he opened the coach door, tossed out the revolver, and stepped gingerly down.

'Waal, what we got here?' The burly Sergeant Jack rode up on his grey, roughly pushing the *haciendado* aside. He peered into the coach, his rifle back in the saddle boot, his heavy Remington revolver at the ready in his left fist. 'Two purty gals and a babe. It sho' is our lucky day, boys.'

Don Miguel held his head high, hatless beneath the fierce sun. 'Please, *señors*, do as you wish to me, but spare my wife and child.'

'Sure.' The black-patched half-breed, Black Wolf, gave a thin-lipped smile, flashing his white teeth. 'First, hand over your wallet and any other gold you're carrying. I know you Mex cattle-barons got plenty.'

'*Señor*, I am not a rich man.' Don Miguel faltered, handing over his wallet. 'I swear this is all I possess.'

'We'll see about that.' Black Wolf leaned forward and snatched a diamond stick-pin from Don Miguel's cravat. 'Empty all your pockets. Don't try to hide nuthin'. Boys, go through them trunks on top. You wimmin inside, get out here.'

The men climbed up, tumbling the heavy trunks to the ground, shooting at the locks, scrabbling through dresses, corsets, stockings, shoes, yelling with triumph when they found a casket of jewellery, necklaces, bracelets, ear-bobs. But they were obviously disappointed to find there was no hoard of gold.

'Hand it all over,' Black Wolf shouted. 'Put it in the sack. We share out later.'

He leaned forward and tore the ruby brooch from Doña Esmeralda's throat, ripping her dress apart. He studied it, rubbing it on his shirt.

'Very nice. The real stuff.'

'You too, Wolf.' Sergeant Jack grinned his blackened teeth at him. 'Toss it in the sack. Fair shares for all.'

'How dare you, you brigands!' Doña Esmeralda drew herself up haughtily. 'You will pay for this. The American army will hunt you down. You will all be hanged.'

'They been huntin' us a long time with that aim in mind,' Jack grinned. 'But they ain't succeeded yet.'

It was true. All the men were remants of the ill-famed Quantrill Raiders, a

400-strong pack of so-called Confederates who had brought terror to Missouri and Kansas during the war. Such men as Bloody Bill Anderson, Jesse James, his brother Frank, and their cousin, Cole Younger, had been the ring-leaders after Quantrill was killed.

'Gentlemen,' Don Miguel was pleading, 'be merciful to us and we will say no more of this.'

Was it likely that men who had taken part in the little spoken about massacre at the small town of Lawrence, Kansas, when 150 men, women and infants, almost all of the town's soldier and civilian population, had been slaughtered, would be merciful?

'Take that whining runt away from here,' Black Wolf said and, as Don Miguel was marched away by one of the men, he took his bow from his back and fixed an arrow. Doña Esmeralda screamed as he fired it into the *haciendado*'s back. The Mexican grunted his pain, and turned, but his knees buckled when a second arrow thudded into his chest.

'Let 'em think the Apaches did it.' Black Wolf hissed another arrow into Don Miguel. 'OK, boys, the wimmin are yours.'

Doña Esmeralda shrieked her horror and anger, flailing out, hanging on to her child. But Sergeant Jack tore the baby girl from her as the whooping men grabbed hold of the two females, fumbling at their clothes, throwing them to the ground.

Jack was in half a mind to smash the baby's head on a rock, but some half-forgotten sense of humanity came over him as he looked at the little creature staring up at him.

He grinned, jigged her in his arms to make her smile, then carefully placed her back in a corner of the coach, wrapping her tight in her shawls.

'Good luck, kid,' he growled. He stepped out and, shooting his revolver at the sky, roared out, 'Giddap, haaugh!' and sent the horses and the

10

near-empty coach rattling away along the canyon.

He watched it go, and sauntered back to the men who were slavering like mongrels around the shrieking Esmeralda. Black Wolf was busy with the struggling Julia. When the men were through they would cut their throats. There would be no witnesses.

Jack left them to it and wandered along to Don Miguel's body. He knelt down and, with his pincers, ripped open his trousers. Men and women often secreted a pouch of gold down there.

'Aha,' he muttered, ripping the linen pouch from the aristo's pale thigh. He glanced back to make sure he was not being watched and investigated further.

'Just some damn map.' He wiped sweat from his brow and studied a torn and faded parchment. 'No damn use.' He was about to toss it aside when his eye caught the word, in scrawled ink, *Superstitions*, above inverted Vs, obviously mountains, a dotted track showing the way to the X of a cave, which read: 'The mine of Don Peralta'.

'Shee-it!' Jack glanced back at the carousing men again, his mouth gaping. 'This is the real McCoy.' He hastily thrust it into his pocket and sauntered back to the others.

'He got anything on him?' Black Wolf paused from firing arrows into the women's bodies, looking enquiringly at Jack.

'Nah. It looks like he must have been as poor as he claimed to be.'

'So, why was he travelling this way under armed guard?'

'Beats me. Maybe to attend a wedding or funeral. You know what they're like.'

'Looks like they attended their own funeral.' Black Wolf grinned at his cheap joke. 'All right boys, you've had your fun. Let's git outa here.'

As Sergeant Jack wandered back to his grey he muttered to himself: 'I ain't tellin' them bastards about this. There must be a fortune in silver or gold in that mine.'

Jesse, Frank, and the Youngers were doing all right for themselves, robbing banks in Missouri. Others of the Raiders had either been hunted down or had taken the oath of allegiance. He and this rag-tag bunch had drifted south to New Mexico where they were joined by Black Wolf, who seemed to think he could take over the outfit. He had led them on into Arizona Territory.

'He's welcome to 'em. I'm tired of these nohopers,' Jack said to himself, as he swung into the saddle. 'I'll give 'em the slip tonight. This is my big break an' I'm gonna make the most of it. Why, I'll be able to buy my own saloon.'

He spurred his horse cruelly, and started after the gang of *viciosos*, leaving the mutilated bodies of the Spaniards to fester in the sun.

2

The sun was rising, a ball of molten fire in the east, silhouetting the dark shape of the stranger who rode out of the Arizona desert. He was an odd-looking cove, thickset, in a battered Lincoln hat, and what looked like a grey, caped greatcoat with sergeant's chevrons on the sleeve, of the former Confederate army, unless the grey colour was just the dust of travel. His baggy trousers were tucked into large boots. A long-barrelled revolver was stuffed into the thick leather belt strapped around his greatcoat. His thin grey horse appeared about ready to drop from exhaustion. They must have travelled a good way, for the nearest stage stop in that direction along the winding dust trail was thirty miles off. The *hombre*'s whiskey-inflamed face in his thick black beard and the curious iron pincers that protruded from his right-arm sleeve, filled the woman who watched his approach with a certain apprehension.

Grace Burgess adjusted the brass telescope she was peering through to get a better view of the stranger. She was at the window of the thick-walled, flat-roofed adobe she ran as a cantina and way station, with changes of horses for the stagecoach that called every two weeks on the run from far-off Sonora to Tucson City. A war widow since her husband had died at the battle of Glorietta Pass, her only companions to help with the work were her aged mother-in-law and nine-year-old son, Ben.

The lonesome cantina and its corrals were set in a valley of rocks, mesquite and sage between two walls of mountains. Fortunately, the native Apaches in these parts were for the moment at peace. But more to be feared were the hard men, the flotsam of war, who were drifting into the territory, generally to escape justice.

'I don't like the look of this varmint.' Grace called to the old woman who was poking an iron into the mesquite coals of their oven. 'Where's my rifle?'

'Who is it?' her son, Ben, asked.

'That's what I aim to find out.' Grace, a willowy, still-attractive woman in her late thirties, put the 'scope aside and reached for the slim Pearson rifle propped in a corner. She took a handful of .32 calibre bullets from a box behind the bar-room counter, and dropped them into the pocket of her pinafore, slipping one into the breech of the single shot. 'You stay well behind me, Ben. We'll see what he wants.'

Her mother-in-law, Rosetta, took a break from poking at the stove, eased her hunched back, her beady eyes bright as she lit a clay pipe gripped in her toothless gums, and puffed smoke out.

'Ain't nuthin' to worry about from one man,' she wheezed out. 'Don't fergit, you got me as back-up, gal.'

'Maybe that's what I'm worried

about.' Grace smiled, grimly. Rosetta tended to go a tad wild when she toted a shotgun! She stepped out into the dawn, holding the rifle across her chest, facing the oncoming man.

Above the doorway of the cantina was a rough piece of oak board etched with the words: WELCOME STRANGER. It had been there since before her time and was what their water hole was generally known as.

'Hey there!' the past-his-prime *hombre* shouted as he arrived and reined in with his good left hand. 'Who's at home in this godforsaken hovel?'

'It's no hovel. It's as good as any place.' Grace, in her long, homespun dress, regarded him steadily. 'Family-run hostelry. How can I help you?'

'All I want's food and drink for me and my hoss.'

'You got cash to pay? We don't do no favours.'

The man's face cracked into a black-toothed grin, and he gave a

17

guttural, coughing laugh. He pointed at the sign with his iron fingers.

'Ain't you s'posed to welcome strangers? Where's your trust in human nature?'

'Times are hard. I ain't got a lot of it no more.' She did not step back or put aside the rifle. 'Let's see the colour of your cash, mister. We seen too many of your sort drifting by.'

'You got whiskey?'

'Sure, we got some in the barrel.'

The stranger licked his fleshy lips, released his reins, and pulled a coin from his pocket. It flashed bright gold.

'You seen one of these afore? Mexican double eagle in pesos worth twenty US dollars.'

'If it's just breakfast and a bottle you want, I don't have change for that.'

'Sergeant Jack's the handle.' The man stayed aboard his worn-out horse, the coin glinting between thumb and forefinger. He looked about him, peering from beneath his top hat at a range of mountains to the west, their peaks flushed by the rising sun at his back. 'Would them be the Superstitions?'

'That's so,' Grace replied. 'Why?'

'I'll be staying a few days. I'll be needing fresh horses, supplies. It's an expedition I'm making — up into them hills.'

Grace gave a scoffing laugh, and brushed her reddish hair back from her brow.

'Gold, is that what you're after? Not *another* crazy man? Those mountains are well named. It's all superstition. There ain't no seam of gold to be found up there. Many have tried and many have failed.'

Ben piped up: 'They say whoever goes looking for it is doomed to die.'

Sergeant Jack regarded him morosely, and growled, 'We're all doomed to die, son. Some sooner than others, thassall.'

Rosetta appeared in the doorway, eager to put in her ten cents' worth, puffing at her pipe.

'I can tell you, mister, many men

have set out looking for that gold. Nobody's never found none and few have returned. Them that did had haunted looks. If there *is* an old Spanish mine they reckon its protected by the ghost of some conquistador. At least, that's all I could make out from their babblings.'

'Ghost of a conquistador! It's you who's crazy. They just say that to scare other folks away from their claim. Them hills ain't never been properly explored and I aim to be the first. Here!' He flipped the gold coin at Grace, who caught it in her palm. 'Where's that whiskey? I got a terrible thirst.'

'Step inside,' Grace replied. 'Rosetta, get him some vittles started. Ben, see to the horse.' She shone the Spanish coin on her dress, her eyes widening. It was a long while since she had seen one of that value. She slipped it into her pocket with the bullets. 'This way, sir.'

'It's sir now, is it? Funny how gold coin makes people change their tune.' The middle-aged drifter swung down from the knock-kneed grey and unknotted a carpetbag from behind the saddle. 'I'll take this. I don't let my belongings outa my sight. I'm like you. I don't trust nobody.' He followed her into the shady, spacious cantina. 'So, where's the man of the house?'

Grace cast a warning glance at her mother-in-law. 'He's away at the moment. Gone hunting.'

'Thass right.' Rosetta tossed a slice of bacon into a frying pan and pushed it on to the stove. 'He could be home any time.'

'Yeah?' The ruffian gave another croaking gasp of laughter and sank down on to a rough wooden chair by a table. 'That so?'

Grace put the rifle aside and knelt to half-fill an empty bottle, turning the spigot of a barrel.

'Fill it, woman,' Jack roared, casting his hat aside and scratching at his balding locks. 'Half a bottle ain't no good to me.'

She did as he bade and took the

bottle across with a tumbler, but Jack snatched it from her, uptilted the bottle by the neck, supping greedily. He gasped as he thumped it down on the table, the copper-coloured liquid already a third reduced.

'Thass better,' he sighed. 'Not a bad bit of stuff.' He glanced at her and reached over to slap his good left hand hard across her shapely rear. 'Neither are you, woman. I've a feelin' I've stopped at the right place.'

'Hey!' Grace spun around, her green eyes blazing, pointing a finger at him. 'Don't you ever do that again. Your gold don't buy *me*.'

Jack grinned gappily at her, then pointed at Rosetta. 'How about the old crone? She'll do me. Could you put them gums to use granny, for fifty cents?'

'Huh!' the old woman shrieked. 'You should be so lucky.'

Grace stuck her finger closer to the ex-soldier's nose, waggling it at him. 'This is a Christian household. We'll give you a bed and board for as long as your money lasts and you behave yourself. But there'll be none of that filthy talk. Or you're out.'

'Sure, lady.' Jack put the bottle to his mouth again. He gulped some more whiskey. 'Don't get in a tizz.'

Suddenly, he reached out, grasped her pointing hand in his good one and, quick as a flash, snapped the curious, iron ratchet attached to his right-arm stump around her wrist, locking it. She screamed and struggled as he dragged her to him to involuntarily sit on his knee.

'Sit still, you wildcat.'

'Let me go!' Grace turned her head away as he tried to kiss her. 'Eugh! You stink!'

Jack was licking his tongue up her cheek when he halted. Rosetta had hobbled across and shoved her shotgun into his side.

'You slimy snake. You put that gal down. She ain't fer the likes of you.'

'You piss off outa this, Granma, or

I'll break her wrist.'

'You do as I tell you, pronto. Or I'll blast your insides out.'

Sergeant Jack grumpily detached the iron pincers from Grace's wrist and, as she scrambled away, moaned,

'Aw, I was only foolin'. Where's my grub?'

'You lowdown polecat, you don't deserve none,' Rosetta cried, backing off.

Ruffled, Grace returned to the bar, glowering across at him.

'One more trick like that, mister, and you're out. I'm warning you.'

'All right, just keep the whiskey comin' and you can keep your virtue. What is this a convent? But you're missing out on some gold. I got more coin where that comes from.'

'Keep it!' As her son came in from attending to the horse Grace called out: 'Ben, stay away from that man. Have nothing to do with him while he's here.'

'Why, Ma? What's wrong?'

'Nothing, just do as I say.'

'Why, Ma, what's wrong?' Jack mimicked. 'Hey, boy, where's your daddy got to?'

'He's dead,' Ben blurted out. 'A hero of the war. He led a charge against Union cannon at Santa Fe. I got his sabre.'

'One of us, huh? The glorious Confederacy. We all suffered for the cause, Ben. Look how I lost my hand. You want to see how my new one works? Us Southern boys ain't finished yet.'

Grace snapped out, 'Keep away from him.'

'So, you're all alone? Two wimmin an' a kid. Not a neighbour for miles. Thass the way I like it. Hey, Ben!' He produced another coin from his pocket, a silver peso. 'You wanna earn this?'

'Doing what, sir?'

'Just keep your eyes peeled and a watch-out on that pass, the way I rode in. You see a 'Pache 'breed, his face half-ruined by a bear's claw, riding this way, you hurry and tell me. Understand?'

'Yessuh.' Ben caught the coin flipped to him. 'I'll do that.'

Grace frowned. 'We don't want no gunplay here. If there's a man after you you'd best be on your way. We don't want your money.'

'Aw, he's jest an ol' friend, thass all. Only I like to be ready. Anyway,' Jack sighed, raising the bottle again, 'I ain't leavin' 'til I'm ready to head into them hills.'

Grace glanced at Rosetta and at her son, and by the looks that passed between them none of them liked the sound of this at all. She beckoned to Ben to follow her into their back bedroom.

'I want you to ride over to the captain's ranch,' she whispered, urgently. 'Tell him what's going on. I don't like the look of this villainous character. I believe he's on the lam. I think there's going to be trouble.'

'What do you mean, Ma, on the lam?'

'I mean I think he's an outlaw. Take a canteen of water, ride fast. You should be there by noon.'

'Right, Ma.' Ben only paused to peer through the bead curtain at the bearded outlaw. Then he darted out of the back door, quickly saddled his pony, sprang aboard and headed away fast across the sage.

'Giddap, Silver,' he yelled. 'Come on, git movin'. We gotta find Cap'n Lynch.'

3

Captain Thaddeus Lynch was sat in a hide and oak armchair in his study at his ranch puffing at a curved brier pipe, and reading a leading article in the Territorial Settler, headlined, GHASTLY SLAUGHTER AT HELL CANYON. Apparently two travellers had come across a six-horse coach galloping towards them containing only an infant. They had retraced its tracks and found the victims of the massacre. It was not easy reading.

Under a cross-head, APACHES OR NOT?, the editor, Joe Wesson, fulminated:

Because two of the victims were scalped, and others riddled with arrows, certain Tucson hotheads immediately jumped to the conclusion that Apaches were to blame. They assembled a vigilante posse and, their cowardice fortified by strong drink, launched a night-time reprisal attack on a sleeping and law-abiding Papago village.

Former army scout, Jock McGhee, doubts strongly whether Apaches were to blame, for the arrows bore Paiute markings; the Paiute, of course, are settled hundreds of miles from here. Nor have Apaches been known to scalp their victims before. 'If it were Apaches they would have been more inclined to raise the baby as their own rather than send her on her way,' he told me.

We heartily deplore the contemptible action of these vigilantes who would have been better advised to consult with the authorities before embarking on their foolish and murderous escapade. Stirring up resentment in this fashion can only lead to trouble for honest sober settlers in the territory.

Lynch looked up as his Apache woman housekeeper bustled into his study with his noonday coffee and biscuits. Maria's nose had been sliced off, a common punishment of an unfaithful squaw, and she had been expelled from her tribe. He clearly remembered how she had come running into the Tucson garrison years before, begging for protection. She had been given work in the army cookhouse and when he retired he had taken her with him, along with two of his scouts, Chollo and Spotted Tail.

'This is a bad business.' The captain prodded his forefinger at the page. 'There could be trouble. You remember Jock McGhee and his bagpipes, Maria? It's good to hear he's still with us.'

'Oh, yah. Jock McGhee, good man. Make terrible noise.'

'He sure did, and probably still does.' Thaddeus Lynch laughed uneasily as she left him. He stirred the coffee and turned his attention to another item on the page.

The main victims of the massacre at Hell Canyon have been identified as Don Miguel Bernadino Pico, from Sonora, and his wife, Esmeralda, the others being their servants as yet unnamed. It is believed that the nobleman was carrying an ancient map of the whereabouts of the legendary 'Lost Mine of the Superstitions' which he planned to sell at auction. The proposed sale had caused considerable interest and several large bids have already been received by a Tucson auction house.

The map was missing, presumed stolen, which provokes speculation that this attack may have been planned in advance. Or could it have been mere chance? There have been reports of a gang of Missouri cut-throats on the rampage on the border near Nogales. They may well have been heading back this way and carried out this callous attack on the hapless Mexicans . . .

'Lost map of Don Peralta,' Captain Lynch muttered.

He chewed on a biscuit, pensively. It would not be an impossibility. These things did turn up from time to time. He himself in his wanderings had come across numerous artefacts from the days of the conquistadores. His gaze turned to a Spanish helmet and a pock-marked long-sword which decorated his study walls, amid souvenirs of his Indian campaigns, war bonnets, tomahawks and pipes, as well as an array of natural history curios, glass cases containing giant rattlesnakes, tarantulas, stuffed owls and other specimens of bird and reptile life. It *could* be, he mused, suddenly excited. Why not?

Lynch was a ruddy-faced, snub-nosed man, his trim and solid physique belying his fifty years. Military-style, he kept his red hair trimmed close to the skull, but it suited his masculine air. Poker-backed and grey-eyed, he was an odd mixture of soldier and scholar. He had assuaged the loneliness of thirty years spent on America's frontiers with a lively interest in Indian customs and the world's natural science; his now battered volumes of Shakespeare had been the companion of his night-time vigils.

Curiousity prompted him to take down once again a large map of the area, tracing his finger towards the Superstition Mountains which lay behind an area labelled 'largely unexplored lands'. The legend of the lost mine had always fascinated him. It was reliably reported that of various prospectors who went in search of it forty had never returned. The few survivors spoke of a deep mine, its walls shimmering with high-percentage quartz. It was said they appeared unhinged, reluctant to return, talking some nonsense about the cave's ghostly conquistador guardian.

Thaddeus Lynch prided himself on being a man of logic and reason, but he well knew that in that day and age most stout-hearted men and women were, like their Indian counterparts, still terrified of the supernatural. He had to admit that once or twice he, too, had met with experiences that raised the hair on the back of his neck.

Ah, well, he sighed, it was too late for him to go adventuring into that unmapped maze of mountains. He divided his time between running his cattle ranch and writing his memoirs. He got to his feet and went out into the main dining-hall of the adobe ranch house as his ramrodder, Squat Williams, stepped inside in his dusty range clothes and Stetson.

'Some damn fool vigilantes been stirring up the Apaches,' Lynch called to him. 'I guess we better think about setting a night watch again in case some of their young bloods decide to seek vengeance.'

'Yeah, you think that's necessary, boss?'

'Better safe than sorry.'

'There's the kid from over at the

Welcome Stranger arrived to see you. Says he's got a message from his mother.' Squat, a toad-shaped man, gave a broad wink. It was well-known that the confirmed bachelor, Lynch, was more than a tad keen on Grace Burgess. 'Maybe she's invited you to dinner again.'

'I doubt it. Send him in.' Lynch kept a straight face, ignoring the insinuation, and when Ben presented himself, straw hat in hands, remembering his manners, asked, 'Well, what's brought you all the way out on these backtrails? You're a mite young to be venturing out alone.'

'I remembered the way, sir, from when you brought us out here before. I only got lost once, but retraced my steps like you said to do. Ma's worried, Cap'n. There's a man arrived and she thinks he may be on the lam. She tol' me to tell you that.'

'On the lam.' Lynch eyed the boy, curiously. 'Maria, fetch Ben a tumbler of cold lemonade. Can't you see he's had a long ride? What's he look like, this man, Ben?'

'He's got a strange iron claw. He's drinkin' whiskey real hard. He told me to watch out for a 'breed with a ruined face who might be followin' him. He tried to kiss Ma.'

'Kiss her?' Lynch's face froze for it was something he had wanted to do to Grace for some while but had never plucked up the courage. 'What . . . happened?'

'Gran stuck him in the guts with her shotgun and he let Ma go. But she's worried, suh, there could be trouble.'

'Say no more, Ben. Maria, give him a sandwich while I saddle my horse and find him a replacement pony. Yours must be tuckered out, Ben. We'll bring him back another day. Squat, get Chollo and two of the boys. You're riding with me. Bring your carbines and forty rounds each. There might be some shootin' to do. I don't like the sound of this.'

★ ★ ★

Old Rosetta had initially been suspicious and resentful of Sergeant Jack, but when he enticed her to him, plying her with whiskey, she succumbed. It had been a long time since a man had made overtures her way.

Sergeant Jack was worried. And when he was worried he turned even more wildly than was his custom to whiskey. It blurred the fear in his mind and insides, made him feel falsely brave. He realized now it had been a fool thing to do to try to double-cross Black Wolf. The half-Indian knew how to track a man down. His pride would not let him give up the chase.

'I had some half-assed idea I could mount an expedition up into them Superstititions. But I'd need tools, labourers, supplies for at least a month, wouldn't I, gal?'

He jogged Rosetta up and down on one knee as she hooked her bony arm around his neck. He grabbed for the bottle with his free arm and offered her a tipple.

'C'mon, drink up, sweetheart.'

Rosetta glugged like a baby through her toothless gums, going almost cross-eyed at the fiery brew.

'Thass the way. You know how to enjoy yourself doncha, if your mis'rable daughter-in-law don't? Yeah, I shouldn'a done it. I shouldn'a 'bandoned the boys. I weren't thinkin' right. Greed does terrible things to a man. I shoulda taken it into Tucson. I coulda got a helluva price for it.'

'What you talkin' about, darlin'?' Rosetta was prematurely old, she knew that. The fierce southern sun and wind had burned her face into a birdlike skull of wrinkles; her hair was pure white; the loss of all her teeth through malnourishment had given her cheeks a sunken look. Her body was as thin and scrawny as some old broiler. She was only seventy-three, a mere girl, but she looked ninety, if not more. 'You sure like your whiskey, doncha?'

'I sure do, an' I like a purty gal, too. Yeah, thass what I shoulda done. But, it ain't too late. I'll head out of here in the marnin'. Meantime' — he gave her a squeeze — 'let's party.'

'Mother, what *are* you doing?' Grace had bought a sheep from the flock of two passing peons and had been out in the yard skinning, gutting and butchering. She had thrown the innards across the fence for the coyotes. It was messy work and her apron was horribly bloodstained. She had hung the carcass in the cellar away from most of the flies that had zoomed in like visitors from hell. Now she had a leg in her hands which she aimed to roast for their guest's dinner. If he was paying in gold she had to feed him. She had buried Jack's gold coin in the yard — nobody would be able to change it hereabouts — and reimbursed the peons from her tin of scanty savings.

'Why don't you leave her alone?' she shouted at Jack.

'Aw, I don't mind,' Rosetta giggled.

'She only calls me mother when she gits on her high horse. I ain't her mother, anyhow.'

'She's jest jalous,' Jack roared, and hurled the bottle at the open fire where it exploded in flames. 'Jalous of your looks.'

Rosetta screeched with laughter as the whiskey spun her mind and the man's filthy hand fumbled under her skirts, squeezing her bony thigh.

'Ooh, don't! You're gittin' me all hot and high.'

'You're drunk, Rosetta. You both are. I forbid this.'

'Nuts, Grace. You go 'bout your business. I ain't had a man since Hal died thirty years ago an' I ain't standin' up this chance. You can stay an addled old maid if you want. Me an' Jack's gittin' married. He says he'll be a wealthy man.'

'Rubbish, Rosetta. He only wants you for one thing. He'll drop you like a hot brick tomorrow.'

'Who's complainin'?' The old lady

smiled, sucking in her empty cheeks and wrinkled lips. 'C'mon, big boy, why don't I show you your bed?'

'Yee-haw!' Jack yelled, swinging her up in the air in his arms. 'You don't have to show me. You're as light as a feather. Just point the way.'

'Oh, my God! Whatever next?' Grace stared indignantly as he staggered out with her mother-in-law in his arms and lurched into a curtained alcove. But Rosetta was a consenting adult so she couldn't forbid her. She had the mutton leg to cook. She began noisily attending to the fire, trying to cut out the cackles of mirth from the other room. 'Thank goodness Ben's not here.'

Eventually it became quieter as Rosetta's shrieks stilled. It seemed like the two lovebirds were having a nap in there after their exertions.

'I'm really surprised at her,' she whispered, as she fixed herself a coffee. 'I wonder how Ben's getting on?' She was sick with worry about her son, about the whole situation.

Suddenly she heard the sound of a horse's hoofs on the dust outside. She looked up alertly as a man slid in through the bead curtain across the doorway. A black-haired part-Indian, with a ghastly scar across half of his face. Grace gave an involuntary yelp of fear as he put his finger to his lips and shook his head.

Black Wolf pulled off his riding gloves and stepped silently across the dirt floor in his moccasins. He pointed to a glass indicating she fill it. She poured in whiskey and stared into his one eye as if petrified by its fierceness.

'Where is he?' he whispered. 'Don't try foolin' me.'

Grace was at a loss what to say. The man, Sergeant Jack, might be a loathsome, randy, whiskeybreath, but he was a guest in her home. She had a duty to protect him.

'He's not here,' she lied.

Wolf noticed her eyes wander to the Pearson rifle. He went over, picked it up, quietly broke it, saw it was loaded, clicked it shut, cocked it and drawled, 'I'll take a look.'

The big bedroom to the rear was empty. He went across the bar to the small alcove.

'Waal, what do ya know?' He looked down at Jack sprawled across the half-naked old woman who had a blissful smile on her face. He poked Jack's backside with the Pearson. 'You ain't choosy, are ya, pal? On your feet. Pronto.'

'Howdy, Wolf, old fella,' Jack grinned, embarrassed, as he turned, hauling himself and his pants high. 'I been waiting fer ya. Thass why I been passing the time of day with this young lady.'

'Any oasis in the desert. You can't resist it, can you?'

Rosetta fluttered her eyelashes, coyly covering herself.

'It ain't like you think, we're gittin' wed.'

'Sure, Granny, you believe that. This skunk won't be alive to do no marryin' unless he comes up with what I'm here for.' He whipped the butt of the Pearson upwards, smashing it into Jack's jaw, felling him. 'Maybe that will refresh his memory. Where is it, you thieving crablouse?'

'What?' Jack blustered, rubbing his jaw, trying to get to his feet. 'For Chris'sakes give me a whiskey.'

'You leave him alone,' Rosetta shrieked. 'Or ye'll have me to deal with.'

'Spare me.' Wolf beckoned Jack with the rifle. 'C'mon, where's that carpet-bag of yours. I want that map.'

'Map? What map?' Jack flinched as Wolf brandished the rifle at him again. 'Oh, that map. How did you know about it?'

'I can read. It was in the *Territorial Settler* back at the last way station. Five days since you ran out on us, Jack. Everybody knows about it now. I ain't got any time to lose if I'm to find that mine.'

'Where are the boys?'

'Camped up the road some miles

back. Come on, quit the balloon juice. Spit it out.'

'OK, it ain' no use me sayin' I ain't got it. But we can forget about the rest of 'em, Black Wolf. The fewer of us know the better. Gold turns men into animals. It wouldn't do 'em no good. This is for us, Wolf, you and me. We'll be partners. We'll be rich.'

'Yeah?' The unruined part of Wolf's face grinned, wolfishly. 'Right, that's a deal. So fish it out. What you done with your gun?'

Sergeant Jack had ambled out into the bar-room and was standing barefoot in his trousers.

'It's back in there.'

'Good.' Wolf strode back to the alcove and found Rosetta with the big Remington revolver in her hands desperately trying to release the safety. Wolf snatched it from her.

'I'll have that, Granma. And his baggage.'

He returned to the bar, tossing the Pearson away, covering Grace and Jack with the revolver as he dipped into the carpetbag. He wrinkled his nose as he pulled out sweaty socks, a marlin spike, a yellowed and holey pair of long johns, a mouldy piece of cheese.

'Jeez! What else you got in here? Ah!' He found the parchment map and shook it out with one hand to study it. 'Well, whadda ya know? Who'da thought this would be worth a fortune?'

Suddenly Sergeant Jack made a dive for the rifle. Black Wolf crouched and fired the revolver at him. But his aim was marred by Grace's coming up with the shotgun from under the bar. The crashing of the two explosions inter-wove and, as Wolf leaped back pellets peppered the wall.

Jack howled. 'Ow! You stupid bitch, you got me in the ass!'

Black Wolf was back in command, pointing the Remington, arm out-stretched, at Grace's head as she fumbled to release the second barrel of shot.

'Drop it, or you're dead meat, woman.'

Grace stared at him and reluctantly placed the twelve gauge double barrel on the bartop. Wolf turned the revolver back on the whimpering man on the floor. 'Now, Jack, you two-timing piece of offal, you're going to get what you deserve.'

His finger was tightening on the trigger as a voice rang out:

'Not just yet, he ain't. Hold it right there.'

Black Wolf glanced his good eye to one side and saw, standing in the doorway, a bullet-headed man of soldierly bearing, a carbine in his hands. He looked like he wouldn't hesitate to use it, either. Behind him were an Apache Indian in range clothes, and two other men. A squat, bow-legged galoot came in through the back door, a sixgun in each fist.

'I guess you win . . . this time,' Wolf said, with a sneer, and threw the Remington to the floor.

'We do.' Thaddeus took the map from his fingers and glanced at it. 'This looks very interesting.'

Ben poked his head around the doorpost and wriggled inside as Rosetta came out of the alcove, buttoning her dress, and stroking back her white hair. 'You all right, granny?'

'Sure am, boy. I been havin' one hell of a time.'

Lynch glanced at her in a puzzled way, and frowned.

'Are you OK, Grace?'

Grace smiled and nodded at him. 'You came just in time, Thad. I'm sure he would have killed that man. He may be a blaggard but I don't want him dying in my house.'

'Get me a quack,' Jack whined. 'My poor backside.'

'I've a pretty good idea I know who you men are: two of those Missouri scum who've been terrorizing the neighbourhood. I ought to take you into Tucson to be hanged. But I've a ranch to run and I don't have the time.

And I'm not in the army now. In the meanwhile I'm hanging on to this map.'

'Yeah, you would, wouldn't you,' Wolf jeered. 'You're jest as crooked as me or him. Think you can find that mine, do you?'

'*You* can get out. Don't you ever come back this way again. If you do I'll kill you.'

'You can try,' Wolf sneered as he backed out, his hands still raised. 'I'll be back. I don't give up easy.'

'Get out!' Lynch went to the door, watched the 'breed leap onto his mount and head away back up the trail. 'Think yourself lucky.'

'I ain't with them,' Jack moaned, still lying on his belly. 'Please, git this lead outa me. I'm bleeding. It's agony. I never was with them. I just happened along. I never wanted to kill them folks. I pleaded with 'em not to. Thass why I got out. I'm innocent. I swear to you on my mother's grave.'

'Hmm.' Lynch looked down at him, distastefully. 'A likely story. I guess we'll

49

have to get them pellets out of you. Then you can get out, too, you scoundrel.'

'I'll do it,' Rosetta volunteered. 'You relax, Captain. I'll attend to him. He's my fiancé.'

4

Thaddeus Lynch had spread the parchment map out on the top of the bar and was studying it, avidly.

'Francisco de Coronado must have passed very close by here in 1541 when he and his conquistadores marched from Mexico up through Arizona Territory looking for the fabled Seven Cities of Cibola. He believed these cities contained magnificent gold and silver treasure. Coronado never did find them. The biggest wild-goose chase in history. But perhaps he *did* find some gold.'

'That's a long time ago, isn't it, Thad — fifteen forty-one?' Grace said. 'How do you know?'

Captain Lynch coloured up as she pressed close to him to peer at the map.

'I've made my studies. It's a subject that fascinates me.'

'Look here.' She pointed her finger. 'It seems to be signed by Don Antonio de Peralta, dated fifteen seventy-nine.'

'Yes, and he appears to have given directions to the mine in a kind of code. With any luck a man could follow them.'

'But surely, Captain, you're not thinking . . . ?'

'When men get gold-fever there's no restraining 'em,' Rosetta called out, as with a pair of pincers she picked pellets from Jack's backside. 'They're forever lookin' fer an excuse to kick over the traces and go adventurin'. Like that son of mine and husband of yourn who abandoned his woman and child an' went an' got hisself killed in some no-good war.'

'Rosetta, please don't speak about Frank like that. He felt it was his duty to fight for the Confederacy.'

'Confederates! Heck! A bunch of rebels. And what has it brought us? Ruination. It was his duty to defend his home against the 'Pache, not go trailing after that so-called General Sibley and attackin' the God-fearing folk of Santa Fe.'

Grace glanced at her son, for she knew how proud he was of his father's part in that glorious if doomed campaign and of his brave death at the battle of Glorietta Pass. Her green eyes flickered on Captain Lynch for he was a Unionist officer who might well have fought against her husband in that battle.

'That's all over,' she said softly. 'We're one country now under the Stars and Stripes.'

The rotund ramrodder, Squat, grinned at them, while his cowhands, Tex and Hank, looked on. He jabbed his finger at the map.

'You really think this is the genuine article, Cap?'

'I do believe it is. Would you be interested in making an expedition up into those hills, Squat?'

'Captain, please.' Grace caught hold of his arm. 'Haven't enough men lost their lives already looking for that mine? And now those poor Mexicans slaughtered. How many more must die?'

'Hey!' Jack groaned as he lay on the floor. 'That's my map you're talking about.'

'You stole it, you murdering scoundrel.'

'Finders keepers. I found it on a dead man.'

'Yes, after you'd killed him, no doubt. I ought to take you into Tucson and watch you kick the clouds.'

'Oh, yeah?' Jack turned to rest on one arm. 'While you steal my map and go looking for gold?'

Lynch was stymied for moments by the accusation. He was, after all, an officer and gentleman, borne out by his bearing, his clean linen, frock-coat, ridingpants and well-polished, blood-red boots. The vestige of uniform that he retained was his cape and his old, wide-brimmed cavalry hat, with its cross-swords insignia. The whole company watched him, awaiting his reply.

'True,' he sighed. 'I've always been honest and abided by the law. By rights I ought to hand this map into the authorities, too. But my curiosity's got the better of me. I can't help it, Grace, I just hanker for one last taste of action, to see if there's any truth in this, before I settle down.'

'If you ain't handing the map in, then you ain't got no right to hand me in.' Jack's buttocks glistened white peppered with pink as he rolled on to his belly again and let Rosetta resume her ministrations. 'I tell you what, I'll jine your expedition, Cap'n, for half shares. Don't you worry about the map belonging to them greasers. The mine couldn't be their'n 'cause Arizona ain't in Mex territory no more.'

'You, you whiskey-soaked villain. You killed those people in cold blood. Why should I want you along?'

'Aw, I didn't want nuthin' to do with it,' Sergeant Jack wheedled. 'I jest happened to be there. Didn't I save that poor baba, put her in the coach?

Wrapped her in her blankets, I did, and sent her on her way.'

'There's many a bad man seen the error of his ways and come to salvation,' Rosetta cooed. 'Didn't them torturin' heathen of yourn' — she pointed the pincers at the Apache — 'turn from their sinful life under your guidance? Jack only needs a helping hand.'

'And, anyway,' Jack scowled. 'I'd be a useful addition to your party. I know how to fight.'

'OK.' Lynch went across and shook his hand. 'You're on. It's fair shares if we find that mine. But I want one thing made clear. If I lead and finance this expedition I'll be in charge and there'll be army discipline. Everybody will have to obey my commands without question. There'll be no niggling, or cheating, or backsliding. For a month or so we'll be brothers in arms.'

'What about the ranch, Cap?' Squat asked.

'We've just had the summer round-up, sold most of the beeves. We'll take

Tex and leave Hank and Maria. They can cope.'

'Can I come, Captain?' Ben blurted out. 'Let me come, too. I can ride and shoot and look after horses, help get water, light fires.'

'Don't be silly, Ben.' Grace pulled him into her skirts. 'You're just a child. If these men are determined to go on this foolhardy trek into the hills it's up to them. But it's far too dangerous. Anyway, we need you to help here.'

'I'm sorry, Ben,' Lynch told him, ruffling his hair. 'Your mother's right. This is men's work. I couldn't take the responsibility of protecting you. I fear that fellow Black Wolf will not give up. There could well be trouble.'

'That black-hearted bastard and his wolves will be back tonight, mark my words,' Sergeant Jack shouted. 'You've got to be prepared.'

'I'm afraid it's true,' Lynch told Grace. 'These people are the sort who slaughter any who stand against them, of any age or gender, if you'll forgive me being frank, my dear. Maybe you and your family should return with me to my ranch?'

'No, I'm not leaving my home.'

'You're right, gal,' Rosetta squawked. 'It's gonna be like the old days. Get battened down and the powder ready. We're gonna be under seige an' we're gonna have to give them poxy varmints hell.'

'Goodness! Such language! Rosetta, have you gone crazy?'

'Maybe I have, and hot dang, I like it. Come on, Jack, git on your feet, you ain't hurt so bad. We gotta git out the bullet mould and start boiling up lead. Ben, git the shutters closed and the beam across the door. We can take 'em.'

'What about the horses?' Grace cried. 'They might run them off.' To lose the stage-line replacements in the corral was not something to be lightly overlooked.

'Well, we kin hardly bring 'em in here,' said Rosetta.

'Grace, it might be best if I and my

Apache boy hid your horses along up the canyon. Then we could stay outside in the oncoming darkness. We could take the battle to them on horseback. We are more used to guerilla fighting than hiding in houses like this.'

'No, Thad, stay here.' She involuntarily reached a hand out to him. 'I'm frightened for you. You would be safer inside.'

'Yes, but they won't be so safe if we are outside. Eh, Chollo?' He took Grace's hand, pressing it to his lips, blinking his flinty eyes at her. 'If anything happens to us it may be best for you to surrender this map. Throw it out to them and this worthless drunkard with it.'

'Oh no we won't,' Rosetta growled. 'We won't throw poor Sergeant Jack out to those devils. He wouldn't stand a chance. He's one of us now. We stand together. No surrender. We fight to the last breath.'

'Thanks Rosetta.' Jack got gingerly to his feet. 'I never thought to hear any woman plead for my poor, worthless life.'

'You ain't worthless. You got me around. So walk tall, pull yourself together, grab your gun and lend a hand fixing them shutters.'

'And leave the whiskey alone.' Lynch gave him a shove. 'Or you'll be dead before anybody can shoot you.'

'Aw, a drop don't hurt. I need it. It's like oxygen to me.'

Lynch went to the door and peered around.

'C'mon, let's go, Chollo.'

'Hang on, boss,' Squat called. 'I'm comin' with you. We can get a better bead on 'em from outside.'

'Good luck,' Grace called, and watched them drive her horses away into the desert. 'God deliver you through the night.'

She crossed herself, returned inside and slammed shut the big oak door raising the heavy beam across it.

'Right, Hank, you take the east and you, Tex, the west port. Jack can watch the back of the house. I'll stay at the front. Ben and Rosetta, you keep the rifles loaded and the bullets comin'. We'll be OK. We've beat off Apaches afore. We can handle a few Missouri cut-throats.'

★ ★ ★

But Grace didn't feel so sure of herself, none of them did, as the sky changed into roseate hues, dimming into purple twilight. The eerie silence outside was broken by the wailing howl of a jackal. Or was it?

'Here they come,' Jack shouted, making Grace nearly jump out of her skin. 'I got a bead on one of em.'

'Hang on,' Grace cried, going to join him, peering along the sights of his Henry rifle. 'They're a couple of my customers.'

Two peons were jogging towards them on their packjacks, intent on their usual meal and a bottle of tequila.

'We are closed, Manuel,' Grace called

out to one of them. 'If I were you I would get back to your village and tell everybody to close the shutters. There's a gang of *bandidos* about seeking trouble.'

The peons needed no more prompting, but turned their *burros* and scurried towards their village out along the arroyo.

Shortly afterwards, as the full moon began its rise, Hank called:

'This must be 'em. About twenty horsemen approaching. Shall I give 'em a warning shot?'

'Hold your fire,' Grace said. 'Let's hear what they got to say.'

'Watch out for them,' Jack growled. 'Don't be listening to none of their lies.'

The horsemen appeared out of the night, spreading out in a semicircle about forty paces from the front of the house. They appeared to be a motley gang of ruffians, scruffy, nondescript in battered slouch hats, bandannas and dusty topcoats. Most had carbines at the ready in their hands.

'What a collection!' Grace spoke contemptuously. 'The dregs of the frontier.'

'Don't underestimate 'em, or their firepower, lady,' Jack muttered. 'All of 'em, 'cept Black Wolf, fought with Quantrill and Bloody Bill. We led the bluebellies a merry dance.'

'I'm ready for them,' Grace replied, as she watched the one-eyed Wolf nudge his mustang forwards to parley. He was holding his carbine upright, a white rag of truce tied to the barrel.

'Come forward,' Grace shouted.

Black Wolf did so and drew in ten paces from the house. Grace could see his one good eye gleaming in the moonlight as he peered at the gun poking from the front port.

'We don't aim to hurt you, lady,' he drawled. 'It's that thieving scoundrel, Jack, we want. Throw him out with that map he stole from us and we'll leave you be.'

Grace bit her lip and glanced at Jack as he hissed,

'Don't do it, missus. It wouldn't be Christian. Don't betray me, please.'

'I can't do that,' Grace called. 'He's a guest in my house. Be off with you and let decent folks be. We've sent for the cavalry. They should be here any minute.'

'Nearest fort's thirty miles away.' Black Wolf gave a mocking grin. 'Your messenger wouldn't be there yet.'

'Don't be so sure of that,' Rosetta yelled, in her high-pitched quaver. She poked a long-barrelled muzzle-loader musket through a spare port at the front, and wheezed, 'Howja like your ugly mug and your brains, what few you got, to part company with your shoulders, you dang-blasted, one-eyed half-caste?'

'You again, old woman?' Black Wolf's teeth flashed as he smiled. 'You I will hang by your heels over my fire. I give you three minutes to do as I say. Surrender him or we kill all of you.'

He turned his mustang and sauntered it back to join his men. He turned to them again and called in a sing-song voice, 'Come on out, Jack, wherever you are. We are going to get you. It's no use hiding behind the skirts of those women. They can't protect you.'

'Why, that piece of no-good crow-bait,' Rosetta spluttered, squinting along her sights. 'I've a good mind to — '

'Don't!' Grace ordered. 'Give him his three minutes.'

It was the longest three minutes she had ever known. Grace's finger twitched on the trigger of the Pearson sporting rifle. She could easily have drilled the 'breed. But, suddenly, Black Wolf gave a scream and charged away, followed in a cloud of dust by the rest of his gang. Some of them dismounted and ran to take up positions in cactus and rocks. Others sent their mounts charging around the small adobe building and corrals, hanging low, and firing rounds at the ports as they passed.

Because of their speed and the dust they kicked up it was difficult for Grace to get a good aim, and she had to duck back as some of their bullets splintered the woodwork around the port, or hissed past her head, ricocheting around the room. The noise inside the adobe was deafening and the defenders could hardly see each other through the belching, black powder fumes. The bandits in the rocks were laying down a fierce fusillade, but, as Ben and Rosetta reloaded, Grace managed to take shots at the flashes of revolvers and carbines firing outside.

'Got one!' Jack yelled, as a rider toppled from his horse. 'God help me! Allelujah! I killed one of my old mates.'

'One for me, too,' Tex shouted. 'Right through the eyes.'

Amid the confusion and the whistle of bullets striking chips from the adobe, Grace wiped sweat from her eyes and gritted out:

'They ain't havin' my home.' Her face was pale but determined as she, too, took a man out, her heart hammering with panic and excitement.

Suddenly she heard the thudding of something heavy against the solid wood door. She looked across anxiously, but the strut was holding. 'They've got a battering ram.'

'They're setting the stables on fire,' Hank shouted. 'They're trying to burn us out. Where's the Cap'n got to?'

Grace twisted the rifle around and managed to take a shot at the men battering at the door. One of them screamed and slumped to the ground.

'God forgive me,' she cried. 'That's another I've killed.'

'These swine don't need no forgiving,' Jack roared, blazing way with his sixgun as Rosetta recharged the Henry. 'Send 'em to hell!'

Tex ran to cover the door.

'Stand back, Ben boy. We gotta be ready for 'em if they come through.'

If the cantina had been a wooden building they wouldn't have stood much chance, but the thick walls made of sun-dried mud and straw repelled bullets and did not give fire much purchase. But the wide chimney gave access and in a lull in the battle those inside heard a scuffling on the flat roof.

'Somebody's up there,' Hank whispered. 'Maybe they're tryin' to smoke us out, stuffing sagebrush down?'

But no. A stick of dynamite was dropped down the chimney, bouncing off the oven and rolling across the floor, its short fuse fizzing dangerously. Hank threw himself forward, no doubt intending to extinguish it. But he fumbled awkwardly, and was too late. The dynamite exploded blowing him to to atoms, splattering bits of flesh against the walls and people inside.

'My God!' Grace was hurled back by the blast. Dazed, her ears ringing, she got to her feet, her face grimed with powder and blood, staring with horror at the remains of Hank's bloody corpse. 'How dare they? How dare they do this to us?'

Outside Black Wolf and his men turned to face another enemy as they realized they were being picked off out of the darkness. Shots crashed out and several of them were sent flying from their horses. Suddenly, there was the sound of a bugle call and an increased intensity in the firing.

'It's the Captain,' Tex called.

Grace climbed back to the port and looked out to see Captain Lynch, his Apache, Chollo, and the burly Squat, come charging in, firing their revolvers and carbines to deadly effect as they dashed through. The three men reformed and made another charge. Captain Lynch had his sabre in his hand and, standing in the stirrups, was slashing out on either side, cutting men down. In his swirling dark cape and Union hat he looked a wild and impressive figure as he skirmished back and forth about the house.

Whether Black Wolf and his ruffians thought he was the advance vedette of the cavalry, and the Indian his scout, Grace did not know but it looked as though they had had enough. Those on the roof scrambled off as Black Wolf beckoned with his revolver, and his men swirled their horses around with alarm, hauling up their wounded. There was some intermittent shooting before they all galloped off into the night.

'We sure set them varmints off.' Rosetta gave a shrill holler of triumph as she watched Lynch, Squat and Chollo chase after them. 'They won't be back in a hurry.'

5

'What a sight I look!' Grace paused from her efforts to tidy up her house after the battle to peer into a small cracked glass. Her reflection showed her grimed with blood and black powder. 'I must wash.'

She had opened the doors and shutters to let out the smoke, doused the stable fire with buckets of water, returned to scoop up the remains of Hank on a shovel and place them in a reverent heap outside. She gave a grimace of distaste and went outside to the pump.

'Trust a woman to think of her looks at a time like this,' Tex drawled as he cleaned and reloaded his sixgun.

'Aw, heck, she's thinkin' 'bout the captain.' Rosetta grinned gummily, as she relit her pipe. 'Them two's in lurve. Didn' ya see the way she simpered when he kissed her hand. Ach!'

'Like I'm in love with you, eh, sweetheart?' Sergeant Jack bellowed as he took a seat. 'Go fill a jug. That fight's given me a thirst.'

'Love sure *must* be blind,' the lanky Tex opined as he joined him.

'Yeah, never thought I'd fall for a wrinkled old pea of seventy-three. But she sure knows how to make the bed bounce.'

'Once larned, ne'er forgot. Thar ain't much more to do nights in these parts.' Rosetta smiled sweetly as she returned with the whiskey. 'I bin parched of entytainment since my husband died. Dang fool, got kicked in tha head by a hoss. Shoulda bin attendin' to what he was doin'. Grace is welcome to her ditherin' and prayin'. Me, I like to git on with thangs. I ain't stepped inside a church since they carried Hal in feet first. Yep, I'll have a drop of the brew, too. Don't mind if I do. You an' me, Sergeant Jack, we got a lot of catchin' up to do, boy.'

'Yeah.' Jack regarded the white-haired old woman apprehensively. 'Guess thass sure so, Rosetta.'

Grace eyed them disapprovingly. She had combed back her auburn hair and put on her Sunday dress. She carved slices of cold mutton and arranged it on platters.

'It's almost dawn. We may as well take breakfast. We've got a lot of buryin' to do.'

'Hell,' Jack growled. 'I ain't diggin' no holes. Just drag them stiffies out to the rocks. Buzzards need their breakfast, too. An' the sun'll soon bleach their bones.'

They were starting to eat when the captain and his boys returned with the spare horses.

'We've rounded up the mounts of those six outlaws who were killed, put them in the corral. We can sell them or use them as replacements, Grace. No harm in it. They were probably stolen, anyhow. Where's Hank?'

'It was terrible, Thad.' Grace ran to

hug herself into his arms, pointing at the pile of remains outside the door. 'He sacrificed himself to save us.'

'He was a brave man.' Lynch awkwardly stroked her hair, soothing her. For ten years past he had been starved of the touch of a woman, since . . . since *her*. 'I'll say words over him. The good news is we ran into a patrol of the army out looking for those murderers. 'We won't see any more of *them*.'

'You sound mighty confident, Cap'n, but you don't know Black Wolf,' Jack said. 'We, I mean them's, outrun army patrols afore. They'll split up like the 'Pache, assemble later at some other place. Siddown, man, have a sup an' a bite. You must be parched.' He offered him the bottle and Lynch took a tentative tipple.

When they had eaten it was agreed that they should take three of the dead fugitives' horses as pack-horses, go first to the captain's ranch for him to tidy up his affairs, and then into Tucson to buy mining equipment and supplies for the expedition into the Superstitions.

'It will mean a delay and a detour,' Lynch decided, 'but it's necessary. We need to enlist some more men. We've got to be prepared for any eventuality.'

Later, after they had buried Hank's remains and fashioned a rough cross, dragged the other corpses out to the rocks, retaining their guns and ammunition, and were preparing to leave, Captain Lynch led Grace apart to the shade at the rear of the house where humming birds were hovering about cactus blossoms.

'If I return from this expedition I will have a serious question to ask you,' he said, holding her in his arms.

'There's no *if*, you must,' Grace whispered, 'and if the question's what I think it is then the answer is 'yes', Thad.'

'You make me a happy man, Grace. I'll travel with a singing heart and be back as soon as time allows. But, I must tell you, I have had another woman. It was, in fact, something of a scandal, or regarded so by my fellow officers. You see, Bonny ran a gaming-house at Tucson, a house of ill repute.'

'Ill repute?'

'Yes, my misfortune was to fall in love with a madame. Not that we did not have some fine times together. We were engaged to be wed. But, she disillusioned me. I don't blame her, it's just the way she was. She broke my heart, I'm afraid. Now, meeting you, it's being mended.'

'Why, what did she do, Thad?'

'Well, to put it bluntly, I caught her in bed at her saloon with two of my men, lower rank enlisted.'

'Two?' Grace appeared shocked.

'Yes, she was a feisty girl.'

'Well!' Grace gave a gasp of relief. 'I see. So . . . ?'

'Marriage was out of the question. I've had ten years to repent of my foolishness. I'm looking for a decent woman now and I believe I've found one.'

'To tell the truth I heard a vague rumour about this, Thad. I'm glad you've been frank about it. They say this accounts for why you never went higher up the military ladder, that you should have made colonel.'

'Maybe.' Lynch laughed gutturally, clearing his throat. 'But I was always too outspoken. And I struck an officer who made an indecent remark about Bonny. I guess I was lucky not to be cashiered. I was merely removed to some of the more godforsaken outposts.'

'Thad, are you serious . . . about me?'

'Yes. I'm asking you to marry me.' He spoke with a gentle Irish burr to his voice. 'Will you?'

'But what about Ben? Would you raise him as your son?'

'Of course. And, maybe — there's life in me yet — he might have a brother or sister.'

'That would make me very happy.' She closed her eyes, clinging to his strong shoulders as he kissed her. 'Oh, Thad, I don't want you to go, but I know you must.'

'It's not the hope of riches. It's — this sounds odd — it's the historical interest that spurs me. I want to solve this age-old mystery.'

'Go, then, Thad. But come back to me.'

'I'll be back.' He smiled at her, his eyes twinkling. 'I'll even provide a home for that dreadful mother-in-law of yours!'

★   ★   ★

Tucson was a sleepy frontier town not far from the Mexican border, reached only by horseback or stage-coach. Shortly after the Civil War the Union states had, of course, been linked coast to coast by railroad, but in the South the Iron horse had yet to surmount the 10,000 foot heights of Raton Pass, or even reach Santa Fe. The Spanish influence was still strong, with their royal highway, *el Camino Real*, leading in from the south. The US army kept a garrison there, but since Cochise had been persuaded to lay down his arms, most of the fighting force had been sent north to deal with the Sioux and Cheyenne, who were threatening war.

Captain Lynch and his party ambled their horses through the tumbledown gateway of the old adobe city wall, past boxy Mexican houses, grander, if now dilapidated, apartments of the former conquerors, and the ornate cathedral towering over them. Its bell was slowly tolling, calling the faithful to worship. On the dusty main street were false-front stores made of shiplap boards. Piles of rubbish had been thrown out by the residents. At hitching rails were horses and buggies. A few ranchers, their wives and children, were busy loading supplies on to wagons, but otherwise it was intensely quiet. As they passed the casino they could hear drifting through the batwing doors the murmur of voices and the clicking of a roulette wheel.

'That's where all the action is,' Lynch said. 'There's no hotel so gents just sit around all night and day, Sundays included, readin' month-old newspapers, drinking, gaming or whatever else takes their fancy. Home to all the idlers and drifters of the south-east territory.'

'Sounds like my kinda place,' Sergeant Jack muttered, adjusting the revolver in his belt, and hauling in his grey. 'See ya later. I need to wet my whistle.'

'Take it easy on the hooch, man. And keep quiet about what we're up to. We don't want everyone in town to know where we're going.'

'You can trust me, Cap'n,' Jack grinned, clambering down. 'We're partners, ain't we?'

'We'll camp out overnight on the plaza. I'll take your horse with us and give him a feed. We'll get those cholla needles out of his fetlocks. He looks like he needs some decent treatment.'

80

Squat spat in the dust as he watched the ex-Confederate lurch into the Delphic Oracle.

'He's got a real passion for the likker, ain't he? Worthless villain. Do you think it's wise taking him with us? I don't trust him.'

'He can poison himself with rotgut while we purchase what we need. But he won't be getting any henceforth. I guess we've got to take him, Squat. I shook on it, didn't I?'

'I will watch him like a hawk.' Chollo grunted, his face impassive. 'One false move and . . . ' He made a croaking sound and slid his thumb across his throat. 'Ach.'

'Let's hope there won't be need for that.' The captain gave a scoffing laugh as he glanced at a bloated mule lying dead beside the road. 'It ain't changed much here, has it?'

'Why don't the city council have that diseased thang dragged outa here?' Tex asked. 'Clean up this rubbish?'

'Well, you know what they're like,'

Lynch replied. '*Mañana* will do.'

The wide plaza between the cathedral and the governor's mansion, on facing sides, was the camping-ground of muleteers who, with their twenty-strong teams of mules had hauled supplies of fruit and fresh vegetables up from Mexico, or hardware and necessities along from Fort Yuma ferry, the link to California and the west coast. They were sprawled out taking a siesta in the shade.

'Tucson's blessed with an equable climate so we'll be comfortable enough here,' the captain said, as they hobbled their horses and fed them morrals of split corn. From the open hole of a well they hauled out buckets of reasonably clean water and, leaving the Apaches to watch the horses, went to make their purchases in the dry-goods store.

They stepped into a shady clutter of hempen bags of bran and barley, barrels of dried apples, piles of clothing, tinned goods, saddles, bridles, sewing-needles and a corner for general mining equipment.

'How can I help you, gents?' the storekeeper called out. 'You name it, we've got it.'

'We'll be needing pickaxes, hammers, buckets, winches, ropes, shovels, gun-powder, a bag of flour, baking-soda, ten pounds of raisins, a sack of pinto beans, ditto coffee beans, salt, six tins of sugar, a ten-pound tin of dry biscuits, and let's see, two dozen boxes of forty-five ammunition.'

'We expectin' more trouble, boss?' Tex drawled.

'We may have to protect ourselves against more dangerous predators than wild critters. I'm talking of the human variety. We may need every gun we've got.' Lynch lowered his voice grimly. 'There's already been a lot of killing. There may be more to come.'

'Hey, don't frighten him.' Squat guffawed.

'You're the one who's frightened of ghosts,' Tex replied. 'Not me. We'll jest see who gits sceered.'

Lynch frowned at them. 'That's enough loose talk. Start getting this stuff hauled over to the camp.'

'Goin' prospectin', captain?' the storekeeper asked, licking his pencil as he totted up the bill. 'Where you got in mind?'

'I'm planning on poking around those ridges behind Devil's Rock.' Lynch noticed that a couple of shady-looking gun-toting drifters, in tattered macinaws, had followed them in and were standing to one side, obviously eavesdropping. 'They reckon there's copper to be had there.'

'Good idea; you do that, Captain,' The storekeeper sniggered. 'You could start a whole new boom town like Globe.'

'Quite.' Lynch signed a banker's order as payment. 'Good day to you.'

Outside in the intense glare of the afternoon heat he instructed Squat and Tex to haul the sacks and boxes of supplies over to the campground. He himself went back along the dusty street past a funeral parlour, an apothecary's, a blacksmith's livery, and a billiards hall, until he reached a cigar store. He stuffed slim Havanas into a leather cigar-case, and bought a sack of pipe- and cigarette-tobacco.

He strode on his way past settlers in homespun, cavalry soldiers in dark-blue uniforms ambling about. There were also bearded men in top hats and frock-coats, businesssmen of the town. And on the sidewalk, standing in the shade were the two *hombres* from the store, in their battered Stetsons, revolvers jutting from holsters on their hip-slung gunbelts, who watched him through narrowed eyes.

There were always some of those ravens around. The flotsam of the south-west. Thieves, rustlers, gamblers, pick-pockets, mug-hunters, con men, murderers most of them, on the run from some other town, looking to line their pockets by fair means or foul. The main problem about hiring more men would be to find honest ones. But there were good men and bad in every town, and the same applied to women.

Lynch glanced somewhat apprehensively at a large mansion set back in its own grounds. There was the tinkle of a piano and girls' alluring laughter drifted from the open windows. His face darkened. How many times had he stepped in there when he was in command of the garrison at Tucson? Memories of good and bad times when he had been besotted with her. He hurried on his way.

'Let's see what that rascally partner of mine's up to,' he muttered, as he marched across to the quaintly named Delphic Oracle and pushed through the batwing doors.

For a casino there was a strangely restrained atmosphere, more like a gentlemen's club than a gambling hell. Some men were sprawled on horsehair sofas reading torn magazines, others were ranged along a mahogany bar while elsewhere day-long poker games were in operation, and faro and roulette enthusiasts were hunched like dark-clothed crows over gaming tables. They all seemed to converse in low tones as if respecting each other's concentration, the high-pitched calls of the dealers singing out: 'Place your bets, gen'lemen.'

A fat lady with a harp was seated on a podium plucking gentle, heavenly melodies. All in all it was very restful.

In one corner was sat a peon whose job appeared to be to endlessly tug back and forth on a rope attached to a big fan on the ceiling to keep its two huge blades flapping back and forth and circulate some air through the canopy of cigar smoke. A curious contraption, it was suspended by a rope through a pulley on the ceiling; this rope was attached to a nail in the wall by the bar. Presumably it could be unhitched and lowered if in need of repair.

'Hey!' Captain Lynch slapped his hand on the back of another curiosity sitting at the bar on a stool, his lanky legs in tartan trousers, a tam-o'-shanter pulled down over his bony nose. 'I might have known I'd find you here.'

Jock McGhee spluttered over the cutglass tumbler in his fist. 'Watch it, mon! You nearly made me spill my whuskey.' His eyes were fierce under bristling brows as he turned to see who had the effrontery to disturb him, but softened and sparkled when they saw Lynch. 'Captain, by the devil! A long time it's been. What brings ye back to this sinful city?'

Lynch tapped his nose with a finger to signify secrecy.

'Business, Jock. What's the whiskey like?'

'Och, the usual filthy firewater. What wouldn't I give for a glass of real Scotch distilled from the mountain stream? What business would that be?'

Lynch called for a whiskey.

'You've no doubt heard the rumour of a map?'

'Aye, it's disappeared. The town's been buzzing with it. You don't say you . . . ?'

Lynch glanced around to make sure they weren't overheard, and nodded as he sipped at his glass.

'None other. It's here in my pocket.' His grey eyes twinkled with amusement. 'I'm convinced it's genuine, Jock. Would you be interested in checking it out?'

'Captain, if word of this gets out,' Jock hissed, 'ye're askin' to get your throat slit.'

'Apart from my cowhands, four of them, and that ne'er-do-well over there' — Lynch nodded at Sergeant Jack sat in on a card-game in a corner of the saloon — 'the one with the iron hand, you're the only other man I've told.'

'What's a man like you doing in his company?'

'It was he who retrieved the map from those massacred Mexicans — don't ask how.'

'Captain, you're treading dangerous ground.'

'I'm aware of that, Jock. But ain't it good to feel the pulses quicken? I bet your own heart's started pumping. You fancy taking a trip into the hills, Jock? You know them better than any man.'

'You know how many men've died looking for that mine?'

'Yes, and you can add Don Pico, wife, maid, and four *charros* to the list, plus seven others in a battle out at the Welcome Stranger stage-stop in which I participated.'

'You really think yon map's worth fighting for? Come on, mon, there's no mine. These are just crazy rumours.'

'There must be some truth in it. I've got to find out, Jock. You in, or not?'

'Aye, I'm in. I wouldna miss it. Ye're makin' an ould man feel young agin, Captain.'

'Good man. Drink up. Have another.' Lynch called for refills and raised his glass. 'To success, Jock.' He winced at the fiery brew and muttered, 'We're going to need about four more men, both to haul the equipment and for protection. But the story is we're looking for copper. We don't want everybody getting gold-fever or there'll be a stampede up there.'

'Sure, ye've no need to tell me that. Ye'll find men looking for work hanging around Munoz's corral first thing in the morning . . . '

Suddenly, loud curses emanated from the burly Sergeant Jack as he staggered to his feet, took a swipe at a man sitting opposite him with his iron-pincered fist.

'You dirty, cheatin' whoremonger,' he shouted. 'That ace came from under the table.' He gave a roar and hurled the table over on to the accused, a sharp-faced professional gambler in a frock-coat and embroidered waistcoat. 'Don't try those tricks on me.'

But the gambler, as he was sprawled on the floor had another trick up his sleeve, a four-inch, pearl-handled derringer which, with great legerdemain, he slipped into his palm and pointed at Jack's heart.

'You stinkin' cur,' he hissed. 'I'll kill you.'

Before he could fire, however, an explosion crashed out and the derringer spun from the man's grasp. The gambler shrieked, shaking blood from his wounded hand. All heads turned to see who had fired with such alacrity and precision.

Thaddeus Lynch stood, feet firm, two hands grasping the smoking Colt Navy revolver which covered the men at the table. He strode towards to them. 'This man's a valued partner of mine. Nobody's going to kill him. Not just yet, anyhow.'

'Great shootin', Cap'n.' Jack hauled out his own revolver from his belt, thumbed the hammer and pressed it to the gambler's head on the point of finishing him. 'I can deal with this greaseball. It's the last crooked card he'll play.'

Lynch's right fist shot out, connecting with Sergeant Jack's cheek, pole-axeing him. He took the revolver from Jack's hand, emptied its bullets and slipped them into his coat pocket, as he stood over the former Reb, who was shaking his head and roaring curses.

'Get out of here and shut your mouth. You're nothing but a trouble-maker. Go on, do as I say. We'll have no killing today.'

For an instant it looked as if he might have spoken too soon, for behind him a man in a slouch hat and a dusty suit rose from a table in the centre of the room. He had slipped out a Bowie and was raising it, holding it poised to hurl at the Captain's back.

Jock McGhee looked around him, saw the rope suspending the huge fan, pulled a dirk from his belt and slashed at the rope. The wooden contraption crashed down on to the knife-man, flattening him.

'Agh!' the fellow cried, as he tried to crawl from under the broken fan.

Lynch turned, saw what was happen-ing, and snapped, 'Good thinking, Jock.'

McGhee was still sitting on his bar stool. 'That's the gambling man's sidekick. He was about to get you in the back, Captain.'

'Come on, you two.' Lynch hauled the two dazed men to their feet. 'I'm taking you over to the lock-up.'

McGhee finished his whiskey, tucked his personal cutglass tumbler back in his sporran — he swore it improved the liquor.

'I'll come with ye,' he said.

6

A motley bunch were assembled at Munoz's corral, sitting on the rails or leaning against the walls, as the dawn's orchid tints coloured the sky. Sergeant Jack stood waiting for them, his black beard hiding any bruise the captain's fist might have made upon his jaw. He bowed, mockingly, and indicated a couple of characters he had enrolled for the expedition.

'This here's Pedro Martinez.' A Mexican in tattered leathers, who had a gold-glinting leer and half an ear missing from a knife fight, jumped down from the rail and offered a hand. 'He's the best muleteer on the border.'

'You're up early, aren't you?' Thad Lynch said. 'Didn't expect to see you yet.'

'Thass because I ain't been to bed,' Jack growled. 'My jaw ached too much.

I needed the medicine. But, I ain't holding it aginst you.'

'So, how d'ye know he's so great? He wouldn't be one of your pals by any chance?'

'Och, Pedro's OK,' Jock put in. 'I'd vouch for him.'

'And this here's Sam Zabriskie,' Jack said, pushing forward an unshaven older man in an army peaked forage cap and faded grandaddy vest. 'He's explored the Sierra Madre range from north to south.'

'All he's explored is every saloon in the territory,' Lynch gritted out. 'You seen any action?'

'Shiloh to the Siege of Corinth,' Sam wheezed out. 'You name it.'

'In what capacity?'

'Er, cookhouse.'

'We could do with a cook and a muleteer. I'm paying twenty dollars a month, with a twenty-dollar bonus if we find the copper I'm searching for.'

'Copper?' A wiry little Jew named Eli Calisher, in a big black hat and black overcoat which had seen better days, echoed the word, incredulously, as he leaned against the wall among the other men. 'Heard tell you were heading into the Superstitions looking for some lost mine.'

'The Superstitions, maybe, but it's copper I'm after. You interested?'

'Why not? I'll join you.'

But the rest of the ragged bunch assembled at the informal 'labour exchange' glanced at each other and shook their heads, surlily. They were more interested in raising a few dollars shifting manure, picking melons, or working the regular mule trains.

'You think we're crazy?' one called.

A toothy young man, lean, crop-haired and lanky, in a white shirt, buckskin pants and boots, pushed himself forward with his elbows from the wall.

'I'll go.'

'Can you handle pack-horses, swing a pick?'

'Sure.' The youth gave his horsey

97

grin, his hand patting twin nickel-plated Smith & Wessons suspended by gunbelts low on his hips. 'An' I can shoot.'

'Show us,' Lynch snapped, pointing to an empty can somebody had left on a far post of the corral. 'Hit that.'

Before anyone could blink an eye the gangling young hick's left gun was in his hand and blazing lead. The first .44 slug sent the can sky high and, fanning the hammer, he kept it bouncing in the air until his cylinder was empty. He blew down the smoking barrel as the noise of the explosions still rang in their ears.

'How about that?'

'Very impressive,' Lynch remarked. 'What's your name?'

'They call me Lonesome, seeing as I don't much like men's company. Lonesome Jones.'

'Where you hail from?'

'Hell knows, I was raised in a frontier whorehouse.'

Jock McGhee nudged Lynch. 'He's trouble.'

'He can shoot.' The captain extended his hand to Jones. 'You're in.'

'You owe me the price of them six bullets.' The youth gripped Lynch's hand. 'And I could do with another five dollars up front.'

'What for? We're heading out as soon as we're packed.'

'I'll be needing more forty-fours. You all got forty-fives.'

'Fair enough. I'll pay for them. Get four boxes.' Lynch took out his wallet and thrust a greenback into his hand. 'Meet us at the plaza.'

'You trust this sonuvabitch?' Jack asked. 'How you know he'll turn up?'

'Let's say I trust him more than I trust you, you smelly oaf.' Lynch laughed uneasily and slapped some dust out of Jack's coat. 'We'll purchase a couple of mules and get moving.'

'Don't mind me callin' you a sonuva-bitch, son,' Sergeant Jack grinned at Lonesome Jones. 'If you was born in a whorehouse thass what you are, ain't it?'

'Maybe,' Lonesome drawled, 'but don't push it.'

★   ★   ★

Lynch was supervising the packing of equipment on the mules and the horses, seeing they were properly balanced, with a blanket and small mattress beneath the *aparejo*, the wooden saddle. He strongly believed in General George Crook's adage that a company was only as good as its supply train.

'Right, we're all fixed,' he announced, glancing up at the sun. 'Where's Jones gotten to?'

'He's got an eye for the gals, that boy,' Tex said. 'I seen him with a li'l beaut last night in the casino. I bet he's spending your dollars in her bed right now.'

'Yeah.' Jack gave a roar of laughter, as he put a whiskey bottle to his lips. 'I bet he's havin' the time of his life. Ever bin conned, Cap'n?'

'Well, we can't wait.' Lynch permitted himself a rueful grin as most of the men joined in the raucous laughter. 'Mount up, men.' He rode over to Jack, snatched the half-full bottle from his fist, wiped the mouth on his palm and took a swig. 'Yuk!'

'Hey,' Jack protested. 'Thass mine.'

The captain passed it around the other men until it was empty. He tossed it away. 'That's the last you'll get for a while.'

Suddenly Lonesome came running across the plaza, a bandanna around his throat, his gunnysack of belongings and bedroll over his shoulder.

'Wait for me!'

'That's your mount.' Lynch pointed to a sturdy paint bronco. 'Get aboard.'

The youth hitched his bundles across the horn and swung into the saddle, gathering the reins as Lynch rode his lead horse around in a circle and shouted, tersely:

'Right, there'll be no whingeing,

no backsliding, no fighting between yourselves on this trip. You obey my orders, implicitly. You answer to me or Jock McGhee here, my second-in-command.'

'What about me?' Jack protested. 'I thought we was equal partners.'

'You'll do what you're told, too, you cur. If you or anybody else tries stirring up trouble, you'll be dealt with roughly, army fashion. You got that? Right, let's go. Company' — he raised his arm and called out — 'For-ward . . . '

As they trailed out of Tucson they heard a wild cry and a Mexican girl came running after them, barefoot, her skirts pulled up, sprinting across the sand.

'Lonesome,' she cried, 'Don't go!'

The youth looked down at her from beneath the shade of his black Stetson as she grabbed hold of his boot. He frowned and spat out:

'Marie, go back.'

The breeze blew the girl's hair over her tear-streamed face as she hung on to the stirrup, being dragged along, and screamed,

'Don't go, *mi amor*. You know where they're going. Nobody ever comes back. Don't leave me.'

Lynch had put his horse to a fast lope and Jones spurred his, too.

'Get off, Marie.' He kicked out at her and she went sprawling and sobbing into the dirt.

The girl lay there, her breasts half-revealed in her loose blouse, her arm outstretched, imploring, as the men and pack-horses went jogging past.

'Please, don't go . . . '

Tex gave a whoop of delight. 'Ain't that just a tender leave-taking. She's sure got the hots for you, Lonesome. Whadda ya do to these gals?'

Lynch rode on straight-backed, Jock McGhee, in cape, tartan trews and tam-o'-shanter, bringing up the rear, the column heading out through the rocks, cactus and mesquite. Only once did Lonesome look back. The girl was still lying there, a frail figure against the backdrop of the town. He gave her a wave, took a deep breath, and headed on . . . on into the unknown.

★   ★   ★

They all knew it was a hard journey they had undertaken, and the initial excitement of being on the move was chilled by some trepidation. It was a strange mixture of scenery they passed through, urging their mounts and packjacks across the cracked earth of open desert beneath the broiling sun, through huge rocks scattered in profusion as if by some god's hand, across salt flats where dust devils swirled. Day followed day, and, although the Superstitions were, as yet, just a range of blue-purple mountains far off, every man became aware they were entering a vast and awesome emptiness where only the Apache and wild animals survived. At one point they passed through towering cliffs of mesas, or table-topped rocks, standing ruddy and magnificent as they entered their shade, their shapes eroded by The Great Sculptor over aeons of time.

'Some say this sand was once the bed of the ocean,' Lynch remarked as he dismounted and picked up a small shell. 'And this kinda proves it.'

'Aw, we ain't gonna have to walk agin?' Jack groaned, as the men, too, jumped down and began to lead their horses, trudging away after Lynch.

'This is the way we do it in the army,' he called back. 'We ride a while, then walk a while to rest the horses. It's called survival. You'll do the same as us, Sergeant.'

'It ain't fair, I got a bad arm.' Jack reluctantly dismounted and set off after them, plodding through the dust. 'I ain't used to walking.'

'Save your breath, mon,' Jock said. 'You may be needin' it. We got a fair piece to go afore nightfall.'

'If you ask me,' Sergeant Jack muttered, 'you're goin' to get us all lost. Howdja know where you're goin'?'

'They know.' Jock nodded at Chollo and Spotted Tail who were loping along on either side of Lynch, leading their ponies. 'At least, they know so far. When they get to the Superstitions it might be a different matter.'

★   ★   ★

They made camp that night at the last mapped water hole known as Sulphur Springs. From then on it would be all unexplored lands. The only map they would have would be a barely decipherable scrawl on tattered parchment made, it was said, three centuries before. They roasted a small doe Chollo had stalked and killed with an arrow and feasted on the tender flesh. Lynch had forbidden the shooting of firearms.

'The beauty of arrows is they don't give away your position to the enemy,' he said, 'at least, not until your victim's got one through his neck.' He drew his army cape around his shoulders for the desert nights grew cold and sucked at his curved brier as the stars popped on, staring at the map as if by so doing he would divine its secrets.

'There's got to be gold or silver around here in these hills somewhere.' Jock McChee tapped at rocks with the hammer he carried with him. 'It stands to reason, don't it?' He appealed, one hand outstretched, to the men who were huddled around the flames of their fire. 'Hasn't forty-three million dollars' worth of gold been taken out of California since the 'forty-nine strike? And millions more is being mined in Nevada. There must be a vast seam of gold running underground north to south beneath these great ranges of mountains.'

'Yuh,' Squat agreed, as he squatted cross-legged by the fire. 'But it's finding it that's the trick, ain't it? We've all seen these damned old prospectors been wanderin' for years and barely scratched up enough to keep them in beans. We're probably on the same fool's errand.'

Lynch glanced at the glum faces around him, some nodding assent.

'We don't want none of that defeatist talk, Squat. We've got to think positive. And it's copper we're after, remember?'

Eli smirked. 'Who you kidding?'

Suddenly there was the high-pitched screeching of an owl from out of the darkness and the two Apaches jumped to their feet.

'This place bad spirits,' Chollo grunted, his eyes rolling, fearfully.

Sam Zabriskie gave a howl of derision, imitating the owls. 'Damn fool, 'Pache. They'll make a suicidal charge on a platoon of cavalry, but they're sceered stiff of a hooty owl.'

The Indians, their ragged black hair held by headbands, in their dusty jackets, cotton breechclouts, their muscled, sunblackened thighs bare, with knee-high moccasins, sniffed the night, poised as if to make a run for it.

'We better go, boss,' Spotted Tail muttered.

'That's OK,' Lynch said, raising a

hand to them, and speaking a few words in Apache to assure them that the white man's power would protect them. 'Anyway *we* ain't moving.'

Nonetheless, the two Indians silently picked up their carbines, unhobbled their ponies, and hurriedly left the camp.

'Looks like that's the last we'll see of them,' young Lonesome remarked.

Lynch shrugged. 'They'll be back tomorrow. They'll just find some other place to sleep. At least the bad spirits should protect *us*. No need to keep a watch tonight.'

'It's dang funny, ain't it?' Sam gave his scoffing laugh. 'Another thang Apaches hate is pigs. When we was on the march if we run across a herd of peccaries the scouts used to run 'em down and kill 'em all with their lances, but they wouldn't eat them. They reckoned they were devils from the underworld. They would grimace when they saw us eating bacon. For a laugh I used to show 'em those cans of devilled-ham, you know, with a picture of the red devil Lucifer on top, open one up and offer it. Them 'Pache would back away in terror, their eyes starin'. I allus figgered a tin of ham was better than a six-shot to ward off Injins.'

The men laughed, and Lynch said:

'Sam's got a good point. It's always well to remember the Apache are highly superstitious. They see gods or demons in everything. They live by dreams and portents. I've seen many a war party suddenly change their minds and decide not to attack. Maybe it's their undoing.'

'Ah, you talk a lot of rot,' Sergeant Jack growled, slapping the notched hickory butt of his long-barrelled revolver. 'The only thing that undoes those primitive bastards is this. Their arrows ain't no match for it.' He leaned back on his saddle, wrapped his blanket around his legs and pulled his hat over his eyes. 'I'm gonna git me some shut-eye.'

'I'll stretch my legs and take a look

along at the water hole.' Lynch got to his feet. 'Coming, Jock?'

The moon had risen and they slowed their pace when they reached the muddy well, sitting back in the shadow of a rock to watch. 'It always fascinates me, the animals you'll see at these spots,' Lynch said.

'Aye,' Jock whispered, gutturally. 'All beasties need water, except maybe the kangaroo rats and I guess they sift the moisture out of seeds. Here we are, look who's first on the scene.'

A band of mule deer had nervously approached the water, bending down to lap thirstily. But suddenly they started away, scampering back into the darkness. The good reason for their fear was a bobcat who stalked forward, looked around and drank at the pool.

'Looks like a female,' Lynch whispered. 'She's probably got cubs.'

When the bobcat had prowled off after the deer, Jock muttered, 'It's certainly strange, all these creatures and rodents, mice, snakes, lying low in their lairs all day out of the heat of the sun, then at night the desert suddenly comes alive. It's all killing or being killed.'

'Yes,' Lynch agreed, 'and talking about that there's our own battle for survival. What d'ye think of this bunch, Jock?'

'Y'mean, can we trust 'em? Well, that Sam Zabriskie is out for the main chance. Eli's a dark horse, don't say much. Pedro's a fine muleteer, but I've heard tell he's cut a few men's throats. You never can tell with a Mexican. That Lonesome Jones seems a nice kid on the face of it, but he's got a reputation as a fast gun and you don't earn that without proving it. Your two men, Squat and Tex, seem solid enough. But if it comes to gold or silver, if we ever should find any, then you never know. Men change, they go crazy. You can't trust any of them.'

'What, even you, Jock?'

'Och, even me.' He gave a high-pitched cackle. 'I've often dreamed of goin' hame. It would be nice to go rich.'

They sat in silence for a bit and watched as a striped skunk shuffled out of the night and nosed at the water.

'That reminds me,' Lynch said, 'you forgot to mention that other smelly skunk.'

'Och, *him*. Normally, I'd give a man like that as wide a berth as I'd give yon laddie, but it seems like he's a partner so we have to trust him. But, if we do find anything it might be advisable to watch yon Sergeant Jack.'

'My sentiments precisely. At the moment we need them and they need us. It's when we're getting out that trouble might start. Come on, Jock, let's be getting back. We need to move out before dawn.'

7

They had been travelling for two more days, climbing into the higher reaches of the mountains, each man leading a pack-horse, urging them up treacherous trails, when there was a screaming bray of terror. Lynch looked around to see one of the mules half-hanging over the precipice, his back hoofs scrambling to gain purchase and pulling Lonesome Jones on his horse with him. The lanky youth pulled his knife from his scabbard and cut at the taut rawhide rope. With a final squeal of fear the mule went flying back, bouncing and falling some 200 feet to lie beneath its pack amid rubble at the foot of the cliff.

'Whass in hell you do, you fool?' Pedro was incensed. 'You could hung on to him. We would helped you haul him back.'

'He was taking me with him.'

Lonesome's face had visibly paled under his tan. 'It was a near thing.'

Pedro started slinging a string of insults and curses at him in Spanish and broken English as if the loss of a mule was more to him than the death of a man. Suddenly one of Jones's Smith & Wessons was in his hand, the deathly hole pointed at Martinez.

'You shut your mouth, you hear?'

'Hold it!' Lynch shouted, dismounting and making his way back. 'Put that gun away, Lonesome. We'll have no shooting.'

'Go on, keel me,' Martinez jeered. 'Thass all you know what to do, you useless son of whore.'

'Come on,' Lynch said, taking the shaggy head of Lonesome's piebald horse, turning it around, reassuring the startled animal, leading it on. 'Let's get on solid ground before another accident happens.'

'Nobody talks to me that way,' the youth yelled, turning in the saddle to keep the revolver aimed at Martinez.

'Certainly not some lousy greaser.'

'Yeah?' Pedro made a clucking sound. 'Listen to the brave white boy.'

'Move on,' Lynch said. 'Don't rile him, Pedro. Remember, he knows how to shoot.'

'*Sí*, an' I know how to use knife. He not careful one day he get it in hiss back.'

'You quit that talk,' Lynch shouted. 'Or you can go back.'

When they were all safely on firmer ground he peered down into the steep-sided arroyo. 'Those are valuable provisions down there. Someone's going to have to go down to fix a rope to haul them up.'

'Aw, forget it,' Jack shouted. 'We're a mule short now. How we gonna carry it all? Take it out of Lonesome's wages.'

For reply Lynch knotted two lengths of rawhide lariat together and hitched one end fast around a rock. He tested it between his hands as if about to make the descent.

'Hang on.' Lonesome slipped his

116

revolver back in its holster and stepped forward. 'It's my fault. I'll go.'

'That poor critter's still alive. Looks like it's broke its leg.'

The mule was straining its neck to look up, beseechingly. Sam Zabriskie raised his carbine, aimed carefully, and his bullet splattered its brain.

'It ain't now,' he said, drily, as it fell back.

'What the hell you doing?' Lynch roared as the echo of the shot barrelled away along the arroyo. 'Haven't I forbidden shooting? Are you mad? Ye've apprised every savage within ten miles that we're here now.'

Sam eyed him defiantly and spat a gob of baccy juice on to Lynch's boot.

'Wake up, captain. They know we're here. You think they ain't seen our smoke?'

'You'd get fifty lashes for your insolence if we were — '

'Yeah, but we ain't in the army no more. And you ain't a captain no more, are you, Mister Lynch? You're a civilian, no different to me. You ain't gonna be lashing nobody.'

Lynch's pugnacious face reddened with anger as he pushed out his chest and raised his fist.

'You — you scum of the frontier. I should knock you into that gully to join that damned mule..'

'Sure.' Zabriskie grinned. 'But you ain't goin' to, are you, *Captain*' — he accentuated the last word sarcastically — 'because you may be needin' every man you got if it comes to a fight.'

'Shut up, and let's get on with it.' Lynch tried to control his tetchiness. 'All right, Lonesome, you go on down.'

Behind Lynch's back Zabriskie grinned at the others and raised one finger in the air as if wiping it down a board to indicate a point won. But Jock McGhee frowned at him.

'If I were you, laddie, I wouldn't try any more tricks like that or ye'll have me to contend with. A good horsewhippin's what ye need.'

'Aw, go play your bagpipes,' Sam growled and went to sit in the shade.

* * *

After the cursing explosion of temper, recriminations, and the attempt by Zabriskie to humiliate Thaddeus Lynch, it was a relief to the men to leave the hot, dusty plain where pincushion cacti pierced their mounts' legs, and thorns and barbs tore at their clothes. They were gradually climbing into other mountain zones, high above sea level, weaving through a forest of scrub oaks where the air was pleasantly cool. Quail-like plump chickens, with nodding crests, scurried across the open patches, and the two Apaches, who had rejoined them, bagged several for their supper. Here mountain chickadee hopped among the branches.

'Isn't that an Audubon warbler?' Lynch, a keen naturalist, had paused and raised a slim telescope to his eye to study a bird singing high on a tree.

'An Audubon warbler! Hark at him.' Sam tugged down his forage cap and sniggered at the others. 'Who the hell cares what it is? Now what the fugg's he up to?'

The captain had dismounted, taken a pocket compass and a sextant from his saddle-bag. He had laid the parchment map out on a rock, and was peering through the sextant.

'What you think he's doing, mon?' Jock snarled. 'Yon map's marked with latitude and longitude. He's trying to determine our position.'

Lynch turned and regarded them with his flinty grey eyes. 'I think we're on the right track. In fact I'm more or less certain this is the exact route Don Peralta would have taken on his historic march between fifteen seventy-nine and fifteen eighty-one.'

Sam gave a whistle of exasperation. 'So flaming what?'

'So, I think we're on the right track. That's what I said and that's what I mean.' Lynch climbed back on his horse. 'Come on. We've two hours of daylight left.'

Towards twilight they reached a high cliff of black basalt blocking their way. They had to make a search along it before they found a narrow crack of a canyon opening out of it through which a cold stream trickled. There was something eerie and forbidding about the dark slit into which they peered.

'This is it,' Lynch announced, jubilantly. 'Tomorrow we go up through.'

'Och, I don't like the look of that at all,' Jock opined. 'The perfect place for an ambush.'

In twelve days of travelling they had not seen another human, either red or white man. But as the men scrambled around unloading the horses, seeking kindling for a fire, rattling pans and skewers, pounding coffee beans on a rock to tip into their big pot, Captain Lynch walked away from them, extended his pocket telescope and, putting it to his eye, examined the vistas of the way they had come, searching beyond the tops of the forest of oaks down to the lower slopes of the mountains, as a cold mist crept up the canyons.

'See anything, Cap?' Squat asked.

'Not a lot through this mist. But last night I thought I saw a fire back about ten miles or so.'

'You think we're being followed!'

'I don't know. I was hoping to keep this expedition secret, but word has a way of seeping out. Of course, it could be Apaches, but it's unlikely they'd build such a large fire.'

When the quail were roasted and they had sucked on the bones, washing hardtack biscuits down with thick black coffee, they sat around their fire and, as usual, men's thoughts turned to riches. They reminisced about the California farmer who had dug up solid nuggets in his onion patch, the Texan cowboy tossed from his horse into sagebrush full of silver, the grocer in Colorado who had been paid for a twenty-dollar foodbill with the deeds of a mine thought worthless, but which later produced $5,000,000 worth of ore.

'How much you reckon we're going to find, captain?' Eli, who rarely spoke, was hunched in his ancient overcoat with its zinc sheen of age and his black hat, cleaning a powerful saddle-gun. 'You can cut all that crap about copper. We all know we're looking for the lost mine.'

'Well, you'd be a fool not to guess that by now. But we haven't found it yet and if we do, who knows what might be in there? There might be high grade ore. There might be nothing at all.'

'Yes.' Eli stroked the sprinkling of black hairs around his long jaw. 'But what I want to know is if there's ore worth, say, ten thousand dollars, what's our cut?'

'Look,' Lynch replied. 'I'm financing this expedition. Mr McGhee and Sergeant Jack are my partners. You men are strictly my hired labourers. We shook on the terms, twenty dollars a month. If we do strike it rich — and it's a big if — there'll be a good bonus in it for all of you. That's better than sitting on your backsides back in Tucson, isn't it?'

'No, it ain't,' Sam Zabriskie shouted. 'Why the hail should you three take the cream. Why cain't we all be equal partners?'

'Don't be absurd, mon.' Jock gave a hoot of derision. 'What would yon Apaches want with a share? They'd only spend it on whiskey. An' you lot, you'd probably do the same.'

'We'll spend it on what the hell we want to spend it on,' Zabriskie shrilled. 'I'll buy myself the biggest whorehouse in town and drink and fornicate myself into an early grave if I choose. But you'd better get this in your heads: we want our fair share. We're taking the risk, same as you.'

'If I hear any more of this mutinous talk' — Sergeant Jack had got to his feet, brandishing his revolver — 'I shoot the first and last man of you. You men are just hired hands, like the captain says. You better get that into your head, Zabriskie, or it'll be the worse for you. You'll get your twenty dollars and your bonus and that's all you'll get out of me.'

'We'll see about that,' Zabriskie muttered.

'Hang on. Sit down, Jack. Put that gun away. That don't help none.' Lynch looked around the group of men who were hunched around the fire staring malevolently at him: Sam, Eli, young Jones, Pedro, even Squat and Tex, reminding him of a pack of vengeful, hungry wolves. 'You're all getting the fever. That way madness lies. We'll end up back-shooting each other if you go on like this. OK, here's the deal. We'll form a co-operative. Everybody gets equal shares.'

'What, even the 'Paches?' Sam sneered.

'Yes, even the Apaches. Their tribe could make use of it. That's if we find anything. Don't let's get carried away.'

'Wait a minute.' The sergeant waved the revolver in his direction this time. 'I ain't agreed to nuthin' like that. What's Jock got to do with it, anyhow? You an' me, Captain, we're the equal partners. You want to split your half-share you do so. But I'm telling you all now for real, I'm keeping my halfshare.' He rounded on the others. 'Any of you care to argue?'

Lonesome Jones leaned casually back on one elbow and gave his big-toothed grin.

'Who knows? I've a feelin' some of us might . . . '

There was a chilling silence as Jack stared at the youngster, his thumb on the hammer of his Remington, but not daring to thumb it back.

Then Squat spoke up:

'We got to stick together, Sergeant. I'll tell you why, 'cause there's other jackals lurking out there who'd dearly like to get their hands on whatever we get. Stick together or die. Why don't we take a vote on it, Cap?'

'Right, why not? Who's for fair shares?'

Every man, one by one, put his hand up, apart from Jack, who stared at them as if he was about to have apoplexy, 'You . . . you all crazy.'

'Crazy maybe, Jack,' Lynch said, 'but you can abide by the majority vote, or you can get back to the remnants of those Confederate murderers you rode with. And good luck to you.'

'But it's my map. Come on boys, fair's fair.'

'It's our map now, Jack,' Lynch said. 'Agreed, boys?'

Every man suddenly had a gun in his hands and they were pointed in Sergeant Jack's direction. The big burly blackbeard blustered, meeting their eyes.

'Aw, all right,' he eventually said and laid his revolver down on his pack. 'I gotta go ease my guts. You lot make me puke.'

* * *

127

Some while later, when they had stoked up the fire and were rolled up in their blankets, drifting off to sleep they heard a raucous bellowing out in the rocks.

'I'd better go see what that idjit's up to.' Lynch gave a sigh and went in search, guided by a discordant wailing sound. He stumbled upon Jack sprawled half in the creek, croaking a rebel song, his top hat tipped over his nose, a bottle of whiskey wavering in his paw.

'You damn fool.' Lynch hauled him to his feet, taking the bottle from him. 'Where've you been hiding this? You'll have every Indian in the district on our doorstep. They can smell whiskey from twenty miles.'

'Nagh!' Jack wailed, trying to grab it back. 'Don't smash it, Cap'n. It's all I got. I need it, Cap'n, more than a man needs a woman, more than he needs gold.'

Thad looked at the inch left in the bottle. 'Here. Finish it. It's the last ye'll get. Give this poison a rest, man.'

8

'Don't you have the feeling we're being watched?' Lonesome Jones made a kissing sound to urge his mustang through the narrow declivity of the canyon, its walls two hundred feet high on each side. 'Even the dang horses' ears are twitching.'

The men made no reply as they set their mounts splashing along the shallow stream, but all of them appeared tense and nervous.

'At least we know we're on the right trail,' Captain Lynch announced, as they paused to rest their horses at high noon. 'This Black Canyon is clearly marked on the Spanish map. We should soon be out of here.'

He dismounted and studied the cliffs of sharp black basalt. 'These are formed of molten lava of recent origin, probably only two thousand years old.'

'So?' Tex asked, 'what does that mean?'

'It means that this crack appeared in the earth's surface during an upheaval, in other words we're on a fault line. In that case the second clue we have to search for: three large boulders balanced one on the other, pointing the way, may no longer be there. If there's been a 'quake since the map was drawn, which is quite likely, they may have been dislodged.'

'Aye,' Jock added, 'but let's look on the bright side, Captain. They might still be there.'

'True.' Lynch stooped to fill his wooden canteen with water and, turning to glance up over his shoulder at the cliff-top, thought he saw the silhouette of a man against the skyline. But the sun was in his eyes and the figure was no sooner seen than gone. 'I think you may well be right, Jones.' Tight-lipped, his eyes narrowed, he peered up at the cliff but there was no more movement. 'I would be surprised if we were not being watched by whatever savages dwell in these hills.'

'The Hapulchais?' Sam Zabriskie's eyes swivelled with apprehension as he peered up. 'Even Cochise and his 'Paches went in fear of them. Cruel, torturin', godless fiends.'

Chollo and Spotted Tail, too, appeared concerned about being trapped in this shadowy canyon. They spoke to each other, shrilly, in their own tongue with its harsh lisping sounds.

'They are saying we should get out of here quick,' Lynch translated. 'No!' He held up his gloved palm at them. 'We are not going back. We go on.'

'I don' like it,' Pedro said. 'Thees bad place. I don' like whole trip. Bad Indian these parts.'

'Come on,' Sergeant Jack shouted. 'What's a few savages? We're well-armed. What are you, lily-livered girls?'

There was, however, something eerily forbidding about the silent canyon as they made their way up it and Lynch unbuttoned his holster flap, pulling out the revolver and cocking it with his thumb.

'Keep your weapons ready, boys.'

He had no sooner spoken than a flint-tipped arrow hissed past his head and embedded itself in the sand. On the heights of the cliffs darkly silhouetted figures appeared, bows strung taut in their hands.

'Take cover,' Lynch shouted as he raised his Colt Navy .45 and fired at the Hapulchais. But it was a long range for a revolver and, as arrows began to rain down upon them, he swung from his horse, pulled it into the lee of the cliffside, and grabbed his carbine from the saddle boot. A seven-shot Spencer, with an accurate range of 200 yards, it would give him better purchase. The other men, too, were hanging on to their terrified, whinnying mounts, and blazing away at the hostiles; not however, with much success.

'They got us pinned down,' Jock shouted through the explosions and curling gunsmoke. 'There's no real cover, Captain. We'd better make a break.'

Thaddeus Lynch, his seven shots already wasted, saw the sense in this, as the savages suddenly appeared from all points, firing their arrows and dodging back down. If his men took cover on one side of the canyon from the cliff above it made them open targets from the other cliff-top.

'Why don't they damn well stay still?' Sergeant Jack was levering his Henry rifle, with fifteen slugs in the magazine, and firing as soon as a hostile appeared but to no effect. 'I ain't potted one yet.'

Tzit! An arrow sped through the air and nearly took his hat off. In a panic, he hauled himself up on to his grey and yelled, 'Come on. Let's get out.'

One of the Hapulchais, more daring than the others, had leapt down the cliff to stand on a lower rock. Practically naked, he was daubed in red clay and had a spray of leaves entwined in his hair, probably as camouflage. Short and muscular, he held a lance poised in his hand.

In the general exodus to escape, as the white men whipped and cursed their horses up the canyon he hurled the lance to penetrate the chest of Spotted Tail, toppling him from his pony. The Apache scout was left writhing in agony on the ground, hanging on to the lance deep in his chest, as his comrades galloped away up Black Canyon.

Lynch whirled his horse and, arm outstretched, fired his Colt Navy up at the warrior on the cliff. The warrior screamed, and tumbled down almost upon him, thudding into the ground. Lynch looked back at the fallen Spotted Tail, but he was lying still. As arrows hissed about him, the captain returned fire and sent his dun charging away up the canyon.

'There weren't nothing I could do for Spotted Tail,' he said as he caught up with the others. They slowed their mounts, trying to quieten them, out of danger now for the time being. 'We were lucky they didn't kill any more of us, or the horses.'

'They weel try again,' Martinez hissed. 'Be sure of that. Iss true. The Superstition Mountains iss bad luck. I say we go back.'

'Yeah. Thass one down.' Sam looked uneasy, too. 'How many more of us gonna git kilt on this fool expedition? We'll be lucky if any of us get out.'

'That's enough.' Thad Lynch took off his campaign hat to flap flies from his eyes. 'Nobody's going back until we've located this mine. We've ample ammunition and superior weapons. We're not going to let a handful of primitive Indians stop us.'

'That's right,' Jock McGhee agreed. 'Bear up, men. I've brought my bagpipes along. I'll play ye some airs tonight. That should frighten off them superstitious savages.'

'It strikes me you're all crazy,' Lonesome said. 'But if there's gold at the end of this I'm for going on. Come

135

on, boys. The worst you can get is an arrow in the back.'

'Huh!' Zabriskie exclaimed. 'That ain't all. I've seen what these torturing heathen do to a man.'

'OK,' Lynch snapped. 'The sooner we're out of this canyon the better. Let's move.'

★　★　★

By now they were at an altitude of more than 5,000 feet. They emerged from the canyon into a bleak scene of scattered granite rocks and stands of evergreens stretching away to a vista of snow-capped mountain peaks. They took stock of their situation, checking their ammunition, tightening the ropes of the baggage saddles, tending to the horses and looking around them uneasily. But there appeared to be no sign of pursuit. Their attackers had melted away into the maze of rocks.

At night they set guards on watch of their camp, the ten men taking turns, four hours on, four hours off. They were ready to move by daylight and for the next two days spent fruitless hours trailing through the mountains searching for any clues to the old Spanish mine.

'There must be some indications. From what I've read in old books Don Peralta had quite an operation going up here,' Lynch muttered to Jock McGhee, as he puffed on his pipe by the fireside one night. 'He apparently had fifty slaves, mostly Indians, working the deep shaft and carrying the ore back to the south. There seems to have been some sort of mutiny or rebellion. The Indians massacred Don Peralta and most of his men, inflicting terrible casualties on them. Since then little more has been heard except for this legend of the mine's being haunted by the ghost of the conquistador.'

'A lot of poppycock,' Jock opined. 'There has to be a rational explanation. The only spirits I believe in are the liquid variety.' He fiddled with his bagpipes, the mouthpiece to his lips. 'Shall I give us a wee tune to cheer us, Cap'n?'

'No!' Lynch hurriedly put out a hand to prevent him. Jock had played an excruciating dirge the night before. 'I'd rather you didn't. Your music seems to dismay the men more than cheer them.'

'Aye, but it surely keeps the savages away. In the same way it can fill the Sassenachs with mortal dread.'

'Maybe some other time. We'd better try to get some sleep. We're on the graveyard watch.'

'Aye.' Jock groaned, trying to make himself more comfortable. 'What happens if we draw another blank tomorrow. How long we goin' to keep searching, Cap?'

'For as long as the supplies and ammunition last. I haven't come all this way for nothing, Jock. I'm loath to give up.'

'Aye, well there's that wee canyon we passed yesterday. Overgrown with brush. Looked like a box canyon. But you never know.'

'Yes, that's an idea. We'll retrace our steps. I'd a feeling we'd gone too far out of our way.'

'Och, this durn moon. How can a body sleep? It's like a lamp shining in your eyes all night.'

'Yes.' Lynch laughed and pulled his campaign hat over his face. 'But it's good to be sleeping out, ain't it, Jock? Reminds me of the old days chasing Cochise.'

★   ★   ★

Out in the rocks Lonesome Jones was sitting with his back to a rock, his rifle over his knees, keeping watch in the moonlight. Occasionally his thoughts would wander back to the slimly tempestuous Marie. Maybe, if they did strike it rich, he could take her out of the whorehouse. It was no place for a spirited young girl. He had seen first hand what happened to a prostitute when her looks began to fade. Her hopes faded, too. He had seen his mother die in agony from a botched abortion. From the age of thirteen he had been on his own, out on the frontier, without a home, forced to make his own way. And the only way a man coped on the frontier was by fighting his own battles, by expertise with firearms. He had practised repeatedly until he was near precision perfect, but a man never knew when a bullet might come out of the dark, or get him in the back. Or an arrow, for that matter. He peered uneasily at shapes in the moonlight, which appeared to move like skulking Hapulchais. But, no, it was only his imagination. To tell the truth, he enjoyed being out in the moonlight on his ownsome. It made him feel alive, brave, ready for anything. Better than being cooped up at night in some airless room. To see all those stars up there made a man wonder at the strangeness of the universe. He had to admit, though, to be out in these parts at the mercy of torturing hostiles could be pretty eerie.

Yes, he decided, that's what he'd do with his share: buy a *rancho* some place, set up Marie and her family there. It wasn't Marie's fault she was a whore. She had to support her mother and fatherless small sister and brother or they would starve. Yes, he would save her from her sinful life which he knew she abhorred.

The moon had begun its downward course, so he clutched his rifle and slithered on his belly away through the rocks, hoping he did not encounter any night-prowling rattlers, scorpions, or poisonous Gila monsters. He expected to find Sam Zabriskie on watch alone on the point of the rocks opposite him. Sam owned a watch and could tell him if it was time to call it a night. With any luck he might have some baccy left, too. Pedro Martinez must have had the same idea, for he suddenly heard the lisping cadences of his voice. Pedro was not a man he had any liking for and he froze, listening to what he had to say.

'Iss time to get out of here. Nobody hass luck looking for mine. Even if they find they are damned by curse. They all be killed by Hapulchais. I say we take our horses — *vamos* — go!'

'I been thinkin' the same myself. We're goin' higher an' higher into unknown country' — it was the frontier drawl of Zabriskie — 'it's like looking for a needle in a haystack. We ain' nevuh goin' to find this dang fool mine. This expydishun's doomed to fail from the start. How say we go now? Grab the hosses an' go while they're asleep.'

'*Sí*. Maybe we should cut *el capitan*'s throat and take what cash he got?' came Pedro's sibilant query.

'Maybe you got a point. He owes us.'

Lonesome didn't wait to hear more, but wriggled away. He got to his feet and, crouching low, hurried back to the fireside. He looked around him at the sleeping shapes of Lynch, Jock, Tex and Squat. He knelt down and shook the captain awake.

142

'Hey,' he muttered, 'I don't wanna worry you, but I think you got a mutiny on your hands. You better watch your backs.'

'Why?' Lynch shook sleep from his head. 'What's wrong?'

'Well, I don't like to snitch, but I couldn't help overhearing Martinez and Zabriskie just now. They're talkin' 'bout cuttin' your throats and skedaddling.'

'You what?' Lynch hissed. 'You sure about this.'

'Sure I'm sure.'

'What about the others, Eli, Jack and Chollo?'

'Dunno where Chollo's gotten to but Eli's still on watch on the far side. Sergeant Jack's around someplace.'

'Right.' Thad Lynch got to his feet. 'I'll tell the boys. We'll see about this. You back off into the darkness a bit. And Lonesome, thanks.'

The camp was still, the firelight flickering, the four men apparently peacefully asleep, Tex, indeed, giving whistling snores (overdoing it a little), when Pedro and Sam Zabriskie stepped into the camp. The Mexican had his knife in his hand and crept towards the shapes of Captain Lynch and Jock McGhee. He turned and pointed towards Squat and Tex. Sam Zabriskie pulled out his Bowie and nodded. These would be silent deaths. Both were expert at killing men in their sleep.

Pedro stooped down, his left hand outstretched to close over the hat shielding Lynch's mouth, his right hand poised, the knife pointed at Lynch's jugular.

'Oh no you don't.' Lynch's left hand swept up to grip Pedro's knifehand by the wrist and his right fist slammed into the Mexican's jaw.

Simultaneously, Jock came alive, a sturdy stick in his hand which he cracked down across the back of Martinez's head. On the other side of the fire Tex and Squat had thrown their blankets back and leapt on Zabriskie, struggling to disarm him and hold him down. Soon Squat was on top of him, smashing punches into his face.

'You filthy creepin' sidewinder, try to creep up on us, try to kill us, eh?' he panted between blows.

'All right, Squat,' Lynch rapped out. 'Don't kill him. We've got some hanging to do.'

'No,' Martinez shrieked, struggling furiously as Lonesome stepped into the camp. 'You no hang me. No, pliz, it not right.'

'Slittin' our throats is right, eh?' Lynch jutted a revolver into Pedro's guts. 'We better call the others in. They can witness this. Get a couple of ropes ready, Lonesome. This won't take long.'

'No, don't do this, Cap'n. It was the greaser's fault,' Zabriskie pleaded. 'I didn' want no part of it. You can't hang me, Cap'n. I'm an ex-soldier. I fought for my country. Have a heart. Just give me a hoss, let me go. I won't bother you no more.'

'String up the murtherin' spalpeens, Cap'n.' Sergeant Jack had staggered back. 'Thass what they deserve. Good on you.'

Eli Calisher watched in grave silence as Lonesome fixed nooses and slipped them over the heads of the two prisoners. Lonesome sent the ropes spinning over a sturdy bough of a pine and caught the ends.

'You boys better step up on that rock,' he said. 'You'll go quicker that way.'

'You swine. It was you. You *tell* on us.' Pedro tried to kick out at Lonesome with his spurred boot. 'I feex you.'

'It's you who's gonna be feexed, Pedro,' Tex drawled. 'Don' worry, the Cap's gittin' out his Good Book. He's gonna beg mercy on your miserable soul.'

'No, please,' Zabriskie pleaded, visibly shaking, as they stood him on the rock and tightened the rope end to a spur of the tree. 'Don't do this, boys.'

'Don't go askin' for no last requests,' Squat grinned. 'We ain't wastin' a cigarette on your sort.'

'OK, let's get on with it.' Lynch stepped forward, opening the Bible in his hands. 'You men were caught red-handed. The sentence is death by hanging. Everybody agreed?'

All the men, except the hangees, nodded assent.

'But I'm inclined to suspend the sentence on condition you swear on this Bible not to try anything like this again. I will confiscate your weapons, which will be returned only if we are attacked. We will be watching you, you understand?'

Both prisoners gave gasps of relief and eagerly put out their grimy hands to touch the Bible.

'I swear, *capitán*,' Pedro whined. 'I theenkin' crazy in head. I no cause you trouble again.'

'And you?' Lynch clamped Zabriskie's hand down on the Bible. 'You swear on the Holy Bible to stay with us?'

'I swear,' Zabriskie snarled, 'yeah . . . yeah . . . yeah . . . I swear.'

'The only reason I'm doing this is, as

147

you might guess, that we need every man we have, both in case of attack and, should we find the mine, to haul back whatever we find. Think yourselves lucky.'

'We do, Cap. We do. You're a good man. You can trust us from now on.'

'Right. Hogtie them for the rest of the night, Jack.'

'It will be a pleasure. Give us a hand, Lonesome.'

'Then get some sleep,' Lynch ordered, briskly. 'The rest of us will take our turn on guard duty.'

'We sworn we weel be good,' Martinez protested. 'There ees no need to tie us.'

The sergeant kicked him. 'Shut up.'

9

Thaddeus Lynch was straddling a bough of a fallen pine, a small mirror propped in a fork of it before him, taking his morning shave with a cut-throat razor. Military discipline died hard: he liked to keep himself as neat as he could even out in the wilds. He wiped his jaw, trimmed a few stray hairs from around his ears, and called, 'Cut them loose, Lonesome. Give 'em some breakfast.'

It had been a cold night and there was a rime of frost covering the ground. Zabriskie and Martinez were stiff and shivering as their bonds were loosed and they clambered to their feet. As they warmed themselves at the fire, Zabriskie snarled, 'You ain't going to hogtie us every night, are you? What are we, your slaves? You wouldn't treat a dog like this.'

'Most dogs got nicer natures than you, ain't they.' Lonesome said with a grin. 'They don't bite the hand that feeds 'em. You two better think yourselves lucky you're alive.'

'You're free to go if you want to,' the captain snapped. 'Or you can stay. But if you do you'll have to pull your weight. Make your minds up.'

'Yeah, but remember,' the sergeant said, 'Black Wolf and his boys'll be lurking somewhere back there. That 'breed's craftier than a prairie fox and meaner than a rattler when he strikes. I don't go much on your chances. You'd be better off with us.'

Zabriskie eyed Martinez and replied, 'All right, we'll stay.'

'Right, saddle up, boys. We've wasted too much time.'

They trailed back along the rimrock of the mountain until they reached the narrow, overgrown defile leading steeply upwards. They had to dismount and push their way through overgrown branches and brushwood, the sharp scent of *piñon* in their nostrils heightened by the cooler air. After a while they came out on a ledge of rock where the mountain treeline ceased.

'Just look at that, Captain,' Jock McGhee hooted, pointing to two rocks, each some fifteen feet tall, balanced one on the other. 'See that other big one in the brush. It's my guess that's toppled off. That might well have been the three-stone column on the map.'

'Yes, and pointing the way. We may be on to something, Jock. Right, we'll keep on moving upwards through the pass.'

Lynch hauled his ex-army plug onwards and upwards, leading the way, and very soon they emerged upon a bare plateau with a view of great ranges of mountains stretching on into Mexico. 'You can see by the way these rocks have been tossed around there must have been a great eruption of the earth's crust here.'

The band of men stared about them somehow aware of their own puniness in the face of awesome nature. There was no sign of beast or man, no sound except the constant mountain wind tugging at their hats and clothing.

Tex shuddered, as if, as they say, someone had stepped on his grave, or he had had a sudden premonition of his or their, imminent danger. 'It sure is a way-out place. Kinda gives ya the heebie-jeebies.'

'Listen,' Squat intoned, 'it's like you kin hear voices whispering in the wind, threatening us . . . '

'That's why,' Lynch said, 'the Indians believe in the underworld, in sacred places, in demons. Don't worry, Squat, it's all in your head.'

'Don't worry! Listen to our brave captain,' Sam Zabriskie scoffed. 'Don't worry! These Hapulchais, we might not see them, but they are there. They're so secretive a tribe folks know nuthin' about them 'cept they're more primitive, more cruel than any Apache.'

'Yeah,' Sergeant Jack groaned, 'so you keep telling us. What sorta funk you in, man? Where's your backbone? And, for that matter, where's this lousy mine? All I wanna do is git this job done and git back to Tooh-sohn fer a bottle of whiskey.'

'Look at his hand,' Eli Calisher scoffed. 'He's shaking with fear, this coward. He's in as big a funk as Sam.'

'That ain't fear.' Sergeant Jack stared at his trembling fingers. 'That's the whiskey shakes. I cain't help it. Don't call me a coward you no-good li'l Jew, or I'll put you in an early grave.'

'That's enough,' Lynch shouted. 'Don't needle him, Eli. True, if he was one of them who massacred and raped Doña Esmeralda and her party and nearly started another Apache war, then he is a cowardly murderer. But give him a break. He's suffering for his sins now. Delirium tremens isn't something to be taken lightly.'

He frowned at Jack. 'Maybe a few weeks' abstinence might do you good.'

'It's terrible, Cap'n.' The sergeant wiped at the sweat pouring from him. 'I need another drink. Thass all I can think of. And' — he forced a black-toothed grin — 'gold. Come on, I ain't finished yet. Where's this mine, I said?'

The captain stood in his stirrups as the dun splashed urine, and peered up at the nearest mountain peaks.

'We're looking for a peak with a curious X-shaped gully on its side. Right?' He sat back in the saddle and raised his gloved palm. 'Forward!'

'You mean X marks the spot?' Jock McGhee asked as he rode up alongside him.

'No, it's not as simple as that, Jock. But, as far as I can decipher from the map, it's on the slopes of that mountain that the mine is situated.'

They rode on in silence, each man involved in his own thoughts, across the granite slopes towards the snowline of the jagged peaks that reared before them until, late in the day, as the sun was beginning to set behind their backs, Jock McGhee gave a halloo and pointed.

'Well, thank the Lord for that. There it is.'

They craned their heads in the direction he was pointing and sure enough, as they peered across a craggy valley sweeping upwards to the snow-line of the nearest peak they could clearly see a dark diagonal cross of two intersecting gullies etched out in the snow now flushed pink by the sun's dying rays.

'What time is it, Sam?' the captain muttered, as he shook his gold watch and put it to his ear.

'What you wanna know the time fer?' Zabriskie scoffed, pulling out his own tin-encased timepiece. 'Gotta clock in at yer orf-fice?'

'Just answer the question.' Lynch gave him a withering regard and dismounted, spreading out the ancient map on a rock. 'I make it just before six o'clock.'

'Thass right, thass what it is. Five to. So why ask me?'

Thad Lynch ignored him, consulting

his compass and rearranging the map. They had followed the curving line of the plateau between the hills until they were facing due south-east.

'That's right.' Jock had joined him and he pointed out to him their probable position, the childish sun-scrawl depicted on the map, and the pictograph of the Mountain of the Holy Cross. He traced a dotted line from the sun's shape to a point on the mountain slope. There was the Spanish word *sombre* or shade, and the number 6. 'Yes, three more minutes to go.'

The men were still sitting on their horses gaping up at the mountain.

'Oh, lordy,' Zabriskie sneered. 'What's so special about six o'clock? Has he gone loco?'

'You men quit foolin' about and keep your eyes peeled.' The captain again ran his finger along the dotted line which appeared to touch the highest point of a smaller hump-shaped hill in the fore-ground. 'That's it. That's that one, there. We're in the right position. This is

156

a stroke of luck.'

'What's he talking about?' Tex asked.

Jock McGhee hooted with indignation. 'If you had any brains you'd know what the captain means. You see yon humpy hill before us. Where the shadow of that strikes at six o'clock, that's where the mine will be.'

'How you know?' Martinez said.

'It's on the map, dumb-cluck. All of you, keep looking. Make a mental note of where it strikes.'

As the sun lowered, their own shadows lengthened until they were engulfed and the line of shadow ran fast forward up the slopes of the hills before them. 'Now!' Lynch shouted.

'I've got it!' Squat cried, jubilantly. 'Right by that small clump of pines. That's where the shadow of the hump touched. I'm sure of it.'

'Right.' Lynch folded the map and swung, eagerly, on to his dun. 'Let's go. Try to keep your eyes on where it struck.'

'One good thing, Captain,' Jock

McGhee called, as he too climbed back into the saddle and headed after them. 'At least it's well below the snowline. We won't have too stiff a climb.'

By now the darkness had run all the way up to the mountain tips engulfing them in its strange afterglow. 'Let's hope this is it,' Jock muttered to himself. 'For the captain's sake. He's set his heart on it.'

It was not easy to traverse the valley through the scattered rocks and toil up the slope of the mountain, at the same time keeping their eyes on where the shadow had struck. But they pushed their exhausted horses and their lone protesting mule onwards and upwards through the velvety dusk.

'There it is.' Lonesome's sharp eyes had spotted a big rock below the small knot of pines. He raced his mount upwards and gave a whistle of awe as he leapt down and edged behind the big rock, for there before him was the unmistakable dark hole of a mine. 'Come on, Captain,' he hollered.

'Hurry. We've found it.'

The others jumped from their horses and ran to investigate; they crowded around, Lynch striking a sulphur match to cup in his hands, peering into the timber-propped hole.

'Great Jehosaphat!' he cried. 'This is really it. The lost mine of the Superstitions.'

Some of the men were all for going into the entrance shaft straight away, but Lynch silenced them.

'Listen to me,' he shouted. 'Don't go getting goldfever. First we unpack, set up camp, appoint guard duty, feed the horses and ourselves. Try to control your excitement. We'll be needing ropes and lamps.'

'Aw, to hail with that. You ain't giving me no more orders, Captain. I'm gonna be rich.' Tex had found a candle in his pack, and was lighting it. 'You ain't grabbin' it all for yourself. I'm gonna take a look.'

'Come back, you fool.' Jock McGhee tried to grab hold of Tex, but he broke away and disappeared into the shaft. All Jock could see was his silhouette and the wavering glow of the flame. Jock cautiously followed the Texan along the downward-sloping shaft dug into the rock of the mountain. 'It ain't safe, mon,' he shouted.

His voice bounced off the black rocky walls, a hoarse echo, as Thad Lynch caught his shoulder and snapped:

'Don't go further, Jock. These timber struts could be as dry as dust. One false move could bring the whole shebang down.'

The captain's warning came too late. Tex had gone running on in, following the weak light of the candle-flame. He must have stumbled against one of the props that held up the tunnel roof. There was an ominous crack followed by the clatter of a falling pole and a creaking sound . . .

'Get back,' Lynch shouted. 'For Christ's sake, run!'

He himself half-fell as he followed Jock and the others back along the shaft to the open air, running as if the devil himself was after them. And none too soon. As they ran from the mine there was a crashing sound. The whole cave seemed to lurch, and a hail of boulders spurted out, followed by a cloud of dust, as the mouth of the mine collapsed.

The men cowered back, pummelled by falling rocks and half-choked by dust, waiting for Tex to appear. But gradually, as the air cleared, they realized there was no way he could still be alive.

'Aw, Jasus,' Sergeant Jack groaned. 'The mine's claimed its first victim. How many more of us are goin' to go?'

★   ★   ★

'There will be martial law from hereon,' Thaddeus Lynch gritted out, his face grim. 'I will personally shoot any man who disobeys a major order. Any minor infringements will result in a man being docked ten per cent of his share of

161

whatever, if anything, we get from this mine. Is that understood?'

Exhausted by their labours from three hours spent, on top of a day's travelling, digging through the rubble to bring out Tex's corpse, the men sat around their fire in the darkness, surly and unresponsive.

Lynch himself was dust-grimed, stripped down to his red undervest, for he had led the digging, fraught with danger of another collapse as it was.

'I was in half a mind to shoot poor Tex in the legs as he ran forward. A pity I didn't. He might be still alive now and have saved us a hell of a lot of work. In future I won't hesitate if any one of you tries to put our plans at risk. We must work together as a team, or God help us.'

'Hear, hear!' Jock McGhee lit his pipe. 'It's army discipline we need. Poor Tex went mad dog at the thought of gold. I'd never have thought, *him* of all people. But that's what gold does. It could happen to any of us. In the meantime, it looks to me like that fall wasn't too heavy. We've already dug through the worst of it. What we'll be needing to do tomorrow is send a party out to cut pine props, either from the small copse up above us, or back at the timberline. We'll need to reinforce the shaft roof as we go forward. There could be nothing worse than being entombed inside.'

'You're right, Jock. Thank God one of you has got some sense. Now we need to get some rest. We've got a hard day tomorrow. We must still keep the usual watch. Four hours on, and four hours off.' Lynch pulled on his by now filth-stained shirt and cape. 'Cheer up, lads. Pull together and tomorrow might be pay-day.'

10

The captain was very businesslike in the morning, getting picks, ropes, and winches out, sending Lonesome, Jock and Chollo up the slope with pack-horses to the stand of pines which had managed to grow above the timberline in the crevices of rock. The trees would serve a purpose now as pit-props. He handed shovels to Pedro, Sam and Eli.

'Start clearing back the rest of the rubble. We're going to have to shore up the roof of the shaft.'

'So,' Sam sneered, 'what are you gonna do while we do the hard work?'

'I'm going to sort out the rest of our supplies and bring them into the mouth of the shaft for safety.'

'Safety from what?'

'Take three guesses, man.' Lynch turned his back on them and went out to the horses. He did not trust them,

Pedro in particular. He might have confiscated their knives and guns, but a shovel was a handy enough weapon for any man. However, he did not expect trouble just yet. Not until there was anything worth fighting for. They were not exactly bright. The night before Sam had suggested using gunpowder to blast their way into the shaft! But you could never underestimate men like that; they had a natural vicious cunning. 'We'll have to watch them,' he muttered to himself.

The wood party returned with sufficient pine props to make a start. They all hauled them into the shaft and hammered them into place.

'That should hold it for the time being. If we find any really bad places we'll have to do the same again,' Lynch said as they rested and supped at tin mugs of coffee. 'If, and it's a big if, we find anything worth our while then it would be a good idea to go down to the oak forest for props. Pine ain't exactly strong.'

'Waal,' Squat drawled, as he gobbled at raisin-biscuits baked by Sam in an oven made from an empty tin, 'these ain't bad. It's jest as well we didn't hang our cook.'

Zabriskie's Adam's apple bobbed in his scrawny neck at the memory of how close he'd come to having it stretched. He scowled at them, got to his feet, a pick in his hand.

'Come on, what we waiting for? Let's go take a look.'

'Safety first.' Lynch half-smiled at his somewhat ironic words, for mine cave-ins were the least of their problems. He handed out helmets with small lignite lamps built in the front of each. 'This is the latest equipment. It leaves your hands free. Put 'em on.'

Apaches never had any wish to enter any dark hole in the ground where, they believed, the underworld spirits dwelled, nor did they have any great interest in gold. So Chollo was quite happy to remain on guard.

'Right,' Lynch said, 'let's go.'

166

He led the expedition cautiously into the interior of the mine, surprised by how quickly they were engulfed by a thick darkness through which their lamps cast eerie shadows. A strange, claustrophobic silence was punctuated only by the scraping of the men's boots, their laboured breathing, or muffled words behind him, the drip of water or the sudden, heart-stopping creaking movement of rocks above their heads.

They all paused, listening.

'Don't worry,' Lynch's hoarse whisper tried to reassure them. 'You often hear that sound. It don't mean nothing.' He picked up the discarded head of a pickaxe. 'Somebody's certainly been here before us, but how long ago I wouldn't care to venture a guess.'

They had reached the foot of the gradual descent of the shaft. It had got lower so they were forced to bend double. But it now opened out into a wide chamber. The captain and Jock tapped their hammers against its sides but this revealed nothing of interest.

'If there was anything here its all been mined,' Lynch said, his words echoing gloomily off the bare walls. 'Let's see where one of these passages goes.'

There were two narrow holes leading away in different directions. They chose the left-hand one, having to stoop and then crawl along on hands and knees.

'We're there,' Lynch grunted as he hauled himself out into another chamber.

'Whadja mean, we're there?' Sam asked as he joined him. 'There ain't nuthin' here, neither.'

'Patience is a virtue, mon,' Jock hissed. 'We'll find something, never fear. Me nose is virtually twitching. You can always rely on me nose.'

'There's a sheer drop down a shaft here.' Lonesome's voice was awed as he peered down. He leaned over, holding on to one of the props, which snapped under his weight and went spinning and crashing down. There was a splashing sound below as he regained his balance and stepped back. 'Christ!' he whispered. 'That coulda been me.'

'Careful, men,' Lynch cautioned. 'These beams are rotten with age. Don't touch them. We don't want anybody else killing themselves. That shaft sounds to me about sixty feet deep. What shall we do? Go down or up? There's another passageway up on that wall.'

'Well, I don't fancy going down there,' the sergeant growled in his deep voice, looking at the men cowering back from the ledge. 'But how do we get up? We ain't got a ladder.'

'You're the biggest of us.' Lynch grinned at him. 'Looks like you'll have to be our ladder. Pedro, you're pretty wiry. Get up on his shoulders.'

'Why me?' Jack groaned as he tugged his Lincoln hat on tightly. He braced himself against the wall and the Mexican clambered up on him.

'Ees no good. I steel cannot reach it,' Pedro called.

'Lonesome, see if you can climb up on both of 'em. You're the lightest. Here, take this rope. Find something strong to tie it to and we'll haul ourselves up.'

With their help Lonesome managed to climb up on Jack, and on to the shoulders of the Mexican, hanging on to their hairy heads, stepping on buttocks, wobbling, but balancing like a circus act.

'Nearly there.'

'Ouch, you swine. You keeck me in the face!' Pedro cursed as Lonesome made a jump and wriggled into the hole.

The youth hitched the rope around a buttress of rock and tossed it down. They all clambered up. The sergeant was the last to go and was cursing and panting, trying to fix his iron-pincer hand to the rope as he climbed.

'I'm outa condition. Didn't think I was goin' to make it,' he gasped as he reached them.

'There's another kind of chamber

along here, Cap'n,' Jock, who had wriggled on ahead, called back.

'Yeah, let's hope there's somethun there.' Jack sighed. 'I'm beginnin' to think we come all this way fer nuthin'. Wait fer me, boys.' He hurriedly crawled along the passage after them. 'Don't leave me. I don't like the thought of gittin' lost down here.'

What, he wondered, was the commotion going on at the other end of the tunnel?

'Jasus!' Thaddeus Lynch did not often take the Lord's name in vain, but he was standing arms akimbo, staring at the cave walls in the glimmer of their lights, taken aback. 'Would you believe it?' There was no mistaking the dull green glimmer of pure gold. 'We've found it, boys.'

For long seconds the men gathered about him just stood and stared around them at the shadowy chamber. 'Are you sure, boss?' Squat hissed. 'It ain't fool's gold?'

'No question of that.' Lynch had

stepped forward, reaching up with his hammer to knock off a chunk from the wall. 'This is the real McCoy. High-grade ore in its purest form. What do you think, Jock?'

The Scotsman studied the sample quizzically.

'I'm not an optimistic man by nature. I've learned by hard kicks it's best not to be in this life. But, I would agree with you, Captain. Look at that seam of it up there. It must be ten feet across.'

'I'd venture to say that when we get back to Tucson assays of this quartz will show it to be full of coarse gold and worth at least a thousand dollars a ton.' Lynch hammered off another piece. 'All we've got to do now is load up as much as we can carry to take back.'

'OK,' Sergeant Jack shouted, raising his fist. 'I'm staking my claim to this mine. I'm the rightful owner, I tell you. I'm gonna be a millionaire. Don't you boys worry. I'll cut you in a piece.'

'Aw, shut up, you fool,' Jock said. 'Haven't we already agreed? We share

172

and share alike. You better get that into your thick head. Hoots, mon!' He brandished a chunk and kissed it. 'We'll all be millionaires.'

Eli appeared overcome with rapture. He got on his knees and raised his hands to the wall of gold.

'You spoke about those Seven Cities of Cibola, Captain. Hallelujah! This is the end of the rainbow.'

Sam and Pedro glanced at each other greedily, and began frenziedly smashing their pickaxes into the wall, stuffing rocks into pockets, filling sacks they had brought.

'Quit your blubbering, Eli,' Lonesome yelled. 'We've got work to do.'

'All right, boys, we'll take as much as each man can carry today,' Lynch called out. 'Tomorrow we'll set to work for real. We'll need to organize a chain so we can haul it out quicker.'

'Yeah, sure, Cap'n, a chain.' Sam panted as he broke his nails trying to get the chunks of ore into his sack. 'You keep on talkin'. We'll do all the work.'

Lynch was peering up with his lamp at another opening in the wall above the seam. 'There's another passage up there. God knows where it leads. We'll explore it tomorrow. There may be more. This could be bigger than all belief.'

'Yee-hoo!' Sergeant Jack started dancing a jig, waving a chunk of quartz over his head. 'We're millionaires. We're rich.'

'Och, quit yer babbling man,' Jock cautioned him. 'We got a lot to do, a long way to go before we see any cash out of this. Let's get on with it.'

★ ★ ★

'Ain't it good to see the sunshine, the blue sky.' Lonesome breathed in deep the fresh air of the mountainside as the men emerged from the shaft. 'We've been down there longer than I thought. Sun's going down. Look at that eagle spiralling. He's watching us.'

'Aye, and he's not the only one,' Jock

174

replied, ominously.

All the men looked around them, but if there was anyone out there they were not showing themselves. They began emptying their sacks into the basket panniers for the ponies and mule. They stacked them into a corner of the shaft entrance with the other supplies.

'Any sign of anybody?' Lynch asked Chollo.

'No trouble, boss.' The Apache was squatted down, his carbine over his knees. He watched the men with an offhand curiosity. What good were the green, sparkling rocks to anybody? Why, he wondered, did whitemen go so crazy for them? 'I keep good watch. I kill bighorn sheep with bow. I got it roasting.'

'Good man.' Lynch regarded the panniers. They were already a quarter filled. 'In a day or two we'll be ready to head out of here.'

'Sure.' Chollo shuffled a pack of leather playing cards. The Apaches were keen gamblers. They would bet for a pony, a bridle, trinkets, decorations, small change, anything except useless rocks. 'You wanna game, boss?'

Lynch took a long drink of mountain water, and filled a bowl to wash the dust from his face and body.

'Maybe, after supper. Come on, Sam, stop gloating over those rocks. Get that coffee bubbling. You're s'posed to be cook.'

'Aw, I won't be your cook much longer, pal. Anyway, this mutton's nearly done. Smells good. Help yourselves.'

'Hey, couldn't I do with a jug of whiskey!' Sergeant Jack stumbled back and forth about their fire. He was so excited by their find he couldn't sit still. 'We sure got something to celebrate.'

'I feel drunk without whiskey,' Squat said, as they sat about under the stars. 'I feel high as a kite. I been figuring out what to do with my share. I'm gonna head back home to Oregon, start my own lumber business.'

'Maybe I'll go back to New York,

open a store,' Eli said. 'Mind you, I'll live in the best apartment, have coaches and coachmen, maids and servants, a fancy wife, go to theatres, be as good as any nob.'

'A saloon in Tucson is what I want,' Sergeant Jack hollered. 'As much whiskey as I can drink.'

'*Sí*, no more work for me,' Pedro agreed. 'I go back to Mexico, buy a *rancho*, fine horses, wear fancy duds, have a different serving maid every night.'

'One thang about poor ol' Tex being dead,' Sam drawled, looking over at the pile of rocks beneath which he lay. 'It means more for us. The fewer left, the bigger the share-out.'

'Och, that's no way to talk,' Jock tut-tutted. 'The sooner I'm able to choose better company than the likes of you the happier I'll be.'

Chollo joined in. 'All I want is a big black Stetson hat,' he grunted.

'Listen to the stupid Indian.' Sam gave a guffaw. 'He's easy pleased, ain't he? You can have Black Wolf's when we kill him.'

At this the men went quiet. 'You reckon he's followed our trail?' Eli asked.

'Of course he has,' Sergeant Jack roared. 'He's out there watching, waiting. While we do the hard digging he'll be setting his ambush.'

'That's a possibility. We may have some hard fighting before we get this gold back to Tucson.' Lynch looked across the fire at Lonesome. 'How about you, Jones? You haven't said what you'll do with your share.'

'I been thinking about buying myself a thousand-dollar pair of silver-engraved, diamond-crusted forty-fours.' The long-legged youth was toying with a rosary in his hands. 'But, I dunno. Guns only bring trouble. Maybe I'll marry Marie, buy a place for us and her family. You see, I've never really had a family.'

'Marry that whore? You crazy, gringo?' Pedro's gold teeth flashed in the firelight. 'What's that you play with?'

'It's her rosary.' Lonesome grinned foolishly. 'She give it me as a kinda keepsake. It's very precious to her. She says it'll protect me.'

'Huh! Protect you? You gone soft in head, white boy?' Martinez let out a contemptuous bray of laughter. 'What you theenk she do while you seet here? What you theenk she do to those men in sporting house? You crazy. She no theenk of you. She like what she do. I tell you sometheeng, gringo, when I get back I goin' to have that girl, too.'

He began laughingly describing in obscene detail what he would do to Marie or she to him, drooling the words out.

Lonesome sprang to his feet, his .44s in his fists and pointed at Martinez, his eyes blazing.

The Mexican raised his hands and grinned at him. 'What you goin' to do? I got no gun, remember? You goin' to shoot down a poor unarmed Mexican?'

'You shut your filthy mouth,' Lonesome hissed. 'Or I'll shut it for good. You hear?'

He slowly replaced the revolvers in his holsters, turned on his heel and strode off into the darkness.

'What's up with him? Touchy, ain't he?' Jack laughed and, tired of dancing around by himself, went to poke at the fire and sit down among them. 'Mind you, he's got a point. I'm sick of gun-fighting, wanderin', never knowing where your next meal's comin' from or whether you'll be alive to enjoy it. I seen so much killin' in my time it was nuthin' to me. Why, in the war the corpses sprawled along the roadside were no more to me than dead hogs. But I've had enough. It's given me bad dreams.'

'Weren't you at Lawrence, Kansas?' Lynch asked.

'Sure I was. That raid was Quantrill's orders. Them women and kids got caught in the cross-fire. That happens in war.'

'They say you executed the soldiers who surrendered?'

'Sure we did. We used one bullet for two men. Stuck 'em up together against a wall. That was Jesse's idea. Saved ammunition, didn't it? I ain't proud of that raid. But they were Red Legs. There was a lot of hatred in Kansas in them days.'

'Well, I might have my own problems at Judgement Gate,' Lynch said. 'But it sounds like you're going to have a helluva lot more.'

'Aw, I don't believe all that baloney.' Sergeant Jack stretched out his legs and stared at the flames. 'But I ain't no youngster no more. If I git through this I intend to live quietly. I s'pose I only got ten years left at the most, so the quack says. Somethang about my liver must be mouldy and green. I'd like to jest live decent for once.'

'Atone for your sins?'

'Yeah. Guess you could put it like that.' Jack chuckled, self-conciously. 'I might even marry li'l old Rosetta. She's

181

got a good ten years left in her. She might be white-haired and wrinkly but she knows how to treat a man. Yeah, she's quite a gal.'

Lynch laughed. 'Maybe we three should make it a triple wedding?' he suggested, jokingly.

'Sure, why not? The biggest Tucson's ever seen. I might even sign the pledge. We'll invite young Lonesome an' his gal along to jine us in the vows.'

'How about you, Jock?' Lynch asked. 'You got your eye on anybody?'

'Not me. I cain't abide the hussies.' Jock rolled his words with horror. 'A fine trio ye'll look in the cathedral.'

'Well,' Lynch grinned at him. 'You could at least be our best man.'

'Why don't you cut the cackle,' Eli butted in. 'The thing is what are we going to do about this mine?'

'We'll register it,' Lynch replied, 'that's what we'll do, all of us, equal partners and directors. As I'm the more educated of you, maybe I should be chairman, but you can vote me off if you want to. What shall we call ourselves? The Arizona Mining Corporation? How's that sound?'

'Sounds good to me,' Sergeant Jack said, leaning back on his saddle and tipping his hat over his eyes. 'I'll sleep on it.' There was a pause before he added, 'Though, on second thoughts, maybe *I* should be chairman.'

11

There is nothing like gold-frenzy to make a man work hard. They went back down into the black pit the next morning, their picks ringing out on the rock face, shovels crunching as they filled sacks with chunks of quartz, their eyes gleaming greedily in the dim light, sweat streaking the dust on their faces. They took turns, three men working at the mine face, three men working as a human chain, cursing and grunting as they dragged the bulky sacks back through the narrow tunnels to the first chamber.

'How about backing the mule down the shaft as far as he can get?' Sergeant Jack suggested. 'Then we can tie the sacks to a rope from him and haul 'em to the entrance like that.'

'Good idea,' the captain agreed. 'I'll leave you in charge of that part of the operation as you ain't gonna be much good toting a pick or shovel with that claw of yours.'

Thad Lynch, Jock McGhee and Sam Zabriskie took first shift at the gold face, with Squat, Pedro and Lonesome deputed to crawl through the tunnels, blinking like human moles in the eerie darkness, dragging their heavy loads.

They had rigged up a rough ladder of pine poles and cross-struts to ascend the steep face of the chamber to the second passage, and Squat and Lonesome would throw sacks down to the Mexican waiting in the first chamber, who would drag them back to Sergeant Jack.

'How much you reckon all this is worth, Captain?' Jock McGhee took a rest, leaning on his pick, wiping the sweat from his eyes, waving a hand at the thick seam of ore above their heads. 'At a rough guess?'

'Lord knows.' The captain broke off from hacking at the rock. 'Maybe a million. Maybe two. We've still to take a look through that other shaft up there. We'll have to try to pull the ladder through.'

'Two million dollars?' Sam gasped. 'Are you joking?'

'I'm not. Never been more serious in my life. Mind you, we wouldn't be able to get it all out on our own. We'd have to get a properly organized mining operation started. It would take a lot of time and work.'

'In that case,' Jock said, 'it might be worth us selling out to a big company.'

'Yeah,' Sam put in, 'but not fer peanuts like that dang fool Virginny Finney. He sold the Ophir Mine in Nevada fer a bottle of whiskey, an old hoss and a blanket and now it's making millions.'[1]

'No, we could probably get a good price if we hold out,' Lynch agreed. 'But, for the moment, there's enough in these sacks to raise us many thousands

---

[1] By the 1880s the Ophir had shown a profit of $400 million!

of dollars each. That would be enough to make my retirement comfortable.'

'Mine, too.' Jock spat on his hands and set to again with a will. 'C'mon, mon. The sooner we get them panniers filled the sooner we get outa here. We can only take as much as the beasts will carry.'

At the noon break they devoured cold mutton, which they preserved by hanging it in the cool of the mine. Then the captain suggested the three men at the face change places with those dragging out the sacks.

'Aw, that ain't fair,' Sam whined. 'Why should this whiskey-soaked Johnnie Reb have the easy job. It's time he took his turn humping these damn sacks. I can look after the mule.'

'That's enough from you, you li'l toe-sucker,' Sergeant Jack roared. 'How can I do any diggin' with this iron hand?'

'In that case you didn't ought to get a full share.'

'Shut up. That's an order,' Lynch

snapped. 'All right, Jack, you can take over Pedro's job. Sam can handle the mule this afternoon. Pedro can come up to the face and I'll do some hauling. There'll be no arguments. You'll just do as you're told.'

'*Sí*, but why lazy Apache sit there all day with gun on knees playin' solitaire?' Pedro complained. 'Why not he down here?'

'That's enough.' Lynch got to his feet. 'Let's get back to work.'

The sergeant and Sam snarled at each other like dogs, but did as they were bid, Zabriskie smirking with pleasure that he had got the easier job. He, at least, would get a glimpse of sunlight. Being down in the dark all day was beginning to play on all their nerves.

★ ★ ★

The next morning Sam Zabriskie showed them big, raw blisters on his palms.

'I cain't do no more digging, boys. I'll have to stay with the mule.'

'Well, I guess that's fair enough,' Lynch said. 'You would only slow us down.'

'How about heem?' Pedro nodded at the Apache. 'Time for heem to do some work, huh?'

'OK, Chollo. We want you to come down and help today.'

The captain took the Indian's arm and more or less dragged him into the mine. 'There's nothing to be scared of. There's no spooks down here.'

'Look at the Injin,' Sam jeered. 'He's sceered witless.'

Lynch spoke to the Apache in the Athapaskan dialect, assuring him he would be working by his side.

'I've looked after you in the past, haven't I?' Chollo reluctantly picked up a shovel and followed him.

The captain deputed Lonesome to take over duty as guard.

'Aw, why him?' Sam moaned.

'Because he's fast with a gun, that's why.'

Lonesome shrugged as the others trooped back into the mine. He grinned at Sam, who was blind-folding the mule.

'Suits me,' he said.

★　★　★

Lonesome went outside to scout around, but it was uncannily quiet, only the wind whistling and whispering across the bleak terrain, the Superstition Mountain, with its curious crossed gulleys, rearing its snowy peak over him. He sat on the big rock outside the mine for a while, but then decided to go back inside out of the keen wind. He sat on a box in the shaft doorway, his twin .44s loosened in their holsters.

He heard the familiar sound of the the mule being urged back up the slope of the shaft and got to his feet as Sam appeared.

'How's it going?' Lonesome asked.

'How you think? Here's another sack. Don't just stand there. Give us a hand.'

Pedro, who had been deputed to work in the first chamber appeared behind him, a bucket in his hand. 'We need more water. Ees thirsty work down there.' His gold teeth glinted as he sneered. 'How you get the easy job? You the captain's punk, eh, greengo?'

Suddenly the Mexican swung the bucket at the youth's head, but Lonesome instinctively stepped back, putting up an arm to fend it off.

'Aargh!' he cried as the metal cut into his left forearm and he reached for his right-hand gun.

But Sam had picked up one of the carbines propped against the shaft wall. He swung it by the barrel with all his force, connecting its butt hard against the back of the youngster's neck.

'Hunh!' Lonesome grunted and slumped to the ground, out cold.

'Good. That feex him.' Pedro had left his own gunbelt with the supplies while he worked in the mine, as had most of the men. He looked around for it and buckled it on. He pulled out the revolver. 'I feenish him.'

'No. They'll hear you.' Sam buffaloed the youth again. 'He's out. Come on. Quick. Let's get outa here. Help me fix these full panniers on to the hosses.'

Between them they hauled out four of the heavy panniers of ore, straddled two of the pack-animals with two each, tied them secure.

'We got enough,' Sam said. 'They're welcome to what's left. Hurry. We gotta git outa here fast.'

'*Sí*, I had enough. This place bad luck. It geev me creeps. Come on, *amigo*, less go.'

'What we've got's worth thousands.' Sam giggled nervously. 'It'll do fer us.' He hurriedly saddled and bridled his bronco, swung aboard, and set off guiding his pack-horse with a leading rein. 'So long, suckers.'

'*Sí*, so long.' Pedro gave a yelp of glee, spurring his mustang, dragging the pack-mule after him.

Lonesome shook his head as he came to his senses. He stared at the dust.

'What the devil hit me?'

He groped his way to his feet, hanging on to the shaft wall, feeling at a damp patch of blood in his hair.

'The bastards!'

He looked around groggily and snatched up the first rifle he saw. It was Sergeant Jack's heavy Henry, with cartridges in the tubular magazine beneath the barrel. He hurried outside and, looking down the rocky slope from the mine, saw that the two deserters were already more than three-quarters of a mile away, and heading for the bend in the trail.

Lonesome climbed up the big rock to get a better view, lying flat to rest the rifle barrel and hold it firm. He squinted along the sights, took a bead on the back of the leading rider. The sound of the explosion as he fired rumbled off the surrounding mountain walls.

'Missed!' One of the riders had looked around, startled, but both were still jogging on. Lonesome gritted his teeth and levered the trigger guard, expelling the metal-cased, rim-fire cartridge and feeding a fresh shell into the chamber. It automatically cocked the hammer ready for firing. He squeezed the trigger again. *Ker-ash!*

'Damn!' Again he had missed. It was a long range. The two fugitives were now nearly a mile away, frantically putting their mounts to a gallop, intent upon getting around the high curve of mountainside which led down to the black canyon. Lonesome activated the mechanism again, but they were almost out of sight. He needed to get up higher. He jumped down from the rock and, his head pounding, sprinted up the hillside to the pine copse above the mine. He jumped down behind a small boulder. Now they were in full view, if very far off. He rested the barrel, fiddled with the sights. And fired. *Ka-room!* He heard the rifled lead go whistling away.

It seemed like seconds later, when he thought he had missed again, that he saw Sam Zabriskie throw up his hands and topple from his mustang's back to lie still. 'Got him!'

Lonesome levered the rifle once more aiming at the rider in the large sombrero who was charging on his way, dragging his pack-mule with him, not daring to look back. Five more slugs were crashed out. But Lonesome was in too much of a hurry. Or the distance far too far. Pedro Martinez reached the cover of the mountain wall and disappeared.

'Damn him!'

Jack ran from the mine entrance. Working in the first chamber, he had heard the shots and come up to investigate.

'What's going on?' he shouted. The message had been passed back and the rest of the dusty crew were coming out to join him.

'Them two got the drop on me. I got Sam. But Pedro's got away. They took four of the panniers.' He raised the rifle aloft. 'This is some shooter, eh?'

'Yeah,' Jack grunted. 'Old Ben Henry knew what he was doing.'

Captain Lynch arrived, hatless and shirtless, the sun gleaming on the ruddy stubble on his bullet head. 'You say they got four panniers? Hell! That's half of our haul.'

'The thievin' toe-rags.' Jack cursed, long, loud and luridly. 'I never did trust 'em.'

'It was you recommended them.'

'Nah, that was Jock. Anyway, what we gonna do? Go after Pedro?'

'No, he's well away. He will have taken both the mule and the packhorse. I guess it's my fault. I should never have let them two be together. How's your head, Lonesome?'

'Not so bad. Just feel a bit groggy, thassall.'

'You oughta have stitches in that cut, but you'll survive. Well, boys,' Lynch said, 'we got the rest of the day left and plenty more quartz back in the mine. We can make up our loss. We should be able to heft out enough to fill four more panniers by tonight.'

'We've lost two pack-animals,' Jock pointed out. 'How are we going to transport it?'

'We'll use our saddle horses and walk back, if necessary.' The captain grinned at them. 'Tucson ain't so far away. Only about two hundred and fifty miles. Come on, boys, are you game?'

12

'What 'n hell's that?' Sergeant Jack's eyes bulged as an agonized groaning floated to them through the tunnel above their heads.

The men all froze as if a chill had gone down their spines, glancing at each other in the flickering light from the carbide lamps. They had been working all afternoon at the gold-covered face of the second chamber, dragging more sackfuls of quartz out through the tortuous tunnels. Now they were gathered there about ready to call a halt for the day.

Eli Calisher almost jumped out of his skin as the horrible wailing began again.

'I don't like it.' He tossed his shovel aside. 'Let's get out of here.'

'Wait,' Thad Lynch ordered. 'A noise won't hurt us. I'm gonna take a look along there before we go. Where's that ladder?'

'It's a terrible sound.' Jock McGhee rolled his 'r's as he spoke in a hushed tone. 'But the captain's right. Come on, ye lily-livers. Ye aren't going to let him go alone? Just think, there might be more gold.' He propped the ladder up below the passage high on the wall. 'You go first, captain. We'll be right behind ye.'

Even the captain looked a trifle distraught, poised at the foot of the ladder. But his pugnacious Irish features set grimly as he snapped:

'That's either Beelzebub at his feast or a Kilkenny cat on the tiles. Come on, let's take a look.'

'I'm not going up there,' Eli said, and it was not just the dust that gave his face a whitened aspect. His teeth had begun chattering audibly. 'It's the ghost.'

'Don't be a fool.' Lynch cocked his revolver. 'What are you, men or mice? Follow me.'

The hair on the nape of Jock McGhee's neck had prickled too, but he felt bound to support Lynch.

'Come on, Eli, up the ladder. And you, Chollo.'

The Apache looked as scared as any of them, but climbed lithely up after the other two.

'Maybe I'd better stay here,' Jack blustered. 'I ain't good on ladders.'

'Och, no you don't. We've got to stick together, Sergeant. I'll come up after you.'

They crawled through the tunnel, getting to their feet as it widened, the weird wailing screeching through the air at them. As the men stopped, crowding the threshold of a lofty cavern which appeared to be lit by a spectral glow, they gawped, open-mouthed.

'Oh, my God!' Squat was the only one who seemed able to speak. 'Jesus help us.'

A conquistador was seated at the end of the cave. He was in armour, helmet, gorget, breastplate and ironclad legs.

He held a long sword in one hand. It was from him that the uncanny wailing came. Chollo gave vent to a scream of terror and fell on his knees gibbering. Sergeant Jack and Eli made a move to turn and run. The captain caught them by their clothing.

'Hold fast, boys, There must be a rational explanation for this.' But his own voice quavered as he peered closer. 'It's no man in there. It's a skull and a skeleton.'

Suddenly the skeleton was moving, rising, creaking to its feet, its arms raised . . .

'It's gonna get us!' Eli tore himself from Lynch's clutch, and bolted back down the tunnel. 'Run!'

Nor did the others stay to argue with the apparition. They were brave enough men, but the ghastly sight and sound unmanned them. They turned and raced after Eli. All they wanted to do was get out of that black haunted hell. They had truly lost their wits. Little Eli Calisher made a dive to clamber on to the ladder. But, in his haste, he was too fast. He and the ladder crashed back into the chamber with a sickening thump. The others clawed at each other, teetering on the edge, some wanting to go forward, others pulling back. To jump into that dark depth might well mean breaking a leg. Captain Lynch too, had backed away along the passage, his eyes transfixed on the conquistador. His heart was pounding, his scalp prickling, his mouth dry, as he muttered, 'I don't believe this.'

For answer the skeleton gave another gruesome wail.

★   ★   ★

Lonesome Jones, left on guard, had climbed up to the stand of pines. He had mislaid Marie's rosary. Maybe he had dropped it by the boulder when he was shooting at Sam and Pedro. Yes, he found it, and was about to return, when he heard a strange sound coming from out of the pines. He took a look and saw a cleft in the ground, like a badger's hole from which the noise was floating. It was big enough for a man to squeeze into. Curious, he slid in head first, propelling himself down the steep slope of the tunnel with his forearms, guided by a light at the other end.

He slithered down the steep descent which twisted and turned. It occurred to him that this fault in the earth was probably directly above the mine. It could be a dead end or it might be a back entrance to the workings, long forgotten, or known to only a few. The macabre wailing grew louder and his mind filled with the legend of the ghost of the Superstitions. This, he decided, was a fool thing to do. But the tunnel had become so steep he could not prevent himself sliding on through.

Lonesome managed to slow himself down as the tunnel widened into an open cavern. Suddenly he saw before him the figure of an elderly Hapulchai kneeling on a ledge of rock in the half-light and, like some puppeteer, he was tugging on gut-strings held in his fingers. He had his back turned to him and it was he who was responsible for the blood-curdling wails.

The young Lonesome observed this in a matter of seconds as he tried to arrest his descent, but his efforts were to no avail and he was pitched by gravity on to the back of the kneeling Hapulchai. They both tumbled into the cavern, crashing down on to an erect suit of armour, knocking it flying with a noisy clatter. The old Indian's moaning was for real now that he had broken Jones's fall.

A blue light from an earthenware saucer of burning wax gave a shadowy illumination to the high rock walls of the cavern. Disentangling himself from the old man, Lonesome looked up to see Captain Lynch, closely followed by Jock McGhee and Sergeant Jack, burst into the cavern.

'Lonesome!' Jack cried. 'How in hell did you get in here.'

'There's a secret passage,' the youth

said, brushing himself down. 'It's all a trick. There's no ghost. This li'l gopher set it all up. It was him doin' all the wailing, probably to frighten prospectors away from the mine.'

'Or maybe to hold power over his people.' Thad Lynch stood up the fallen suit of armour and stared into the eye sockets of the grinning skull inside. 'This must be the original conquistador, possibly Don Miguel Peralta himself, from three centuries ago. Well, I'll be a monkey's aunt! He was no doubt killed in the mine when the Indians mutinied and has been here all that time since.'

Chollo and Squat were peering anxiously into the cavern and Jock called to them, 'Come on in, boys. The bad spirits have flown.'

The Hapulchai had ceased his groaning but lay looking up at them, fearfully. His long white hair was held by a thin band of hammered gold, his face and sagging body daubed with clay, painted with symbols. There were four golden rings running up the cartilage of each ear, and gold bracelets around his scrawny upper arms. He clutched at his right arm which hung limp and broken.

Chollo gradually regained his courage when he saw the captain carefully remove the helmet and armour from the skeleton, and lay the bones aside. He sniffed and spoke in guttural Apache or perhaps Hapulchai, to the captive.

When the man had whined a reply, Chollo translated:

'He is priest, or holy man. He say you, Captain, have destroyed their god and will be cursed. He say on religious day Hapulchai venture in here to worship the conquistador and be granted some of his shining stones. He say he is mouthpiece of God Conquistador, as generations of holy men have been, and he merely speak his words.'

The shaman was hauled to his feet, and he backed away, pointing his good finger at each one, gabbling his strange words: 'He say all who steal from conquistador are condemned to die.'

'Well, that's debatable,' Lynch said, 'but interesting, nonetheless. This explains a lot of things.'

'What are we gonna do with this monkey?' Squat asked.

'We'll take him with us. Keep him as a hostage,' the captain replied. 'And, I'm taking this sword and suit of armour, too. This is of more value to me than any damned gold.'

'Heck!' Jock gave a whoop of glee. 'Would you believe it? Who'd have thought we'd all be afeared of a little fellow like this?'

'You might be more int'rested in old armour, Cap'n, but I ain't,' Jack growled. 'You bluebelly officers git a good pension, doncha? But I don't. And if my eyes don't fool me there's more gold up around these walls.'

'There well may be,' Jock agreed. 'But it will have to stay there for now. Come on, let's get back, see how Eli is.'

They lowered themselves down by rope into the second chamber but there was no sign of the fallen Jew. However, they found him cowering outside the cave entrance waiting their return.

'Ye don't know what ye've been missing, laddie,' Jock called. 'Look who we've found. The man behind it all. It was a hoax, mon!'

★ ★ ★

In the morning Captain Lynch gave the order to pack up the horses with what gold quartz they had and move out. When he was satisfied with the arrangement of the panniers, he called, 'Right, we'll have a quick spot of breakfast before we go.'

Firewood was scarce in that bleak zone and Eli had been dispatched up to the copse to see what he could collect. Suddenly they heard a bloodchilling scream followed by more hideous screams.

'What the devil's going on?' Lynch

said, drawing his Colt Navy revolver. 'Oh, my god!'

Two Hapulchai warriors had stepped out from the stand of pines. They were wearing skirts of ragged red cloth, leggings and moccasins of buckskin, otherwise they were naked but for daubed warpaint. Their hair was dressed with red clay and wound in snakelike coils, giving their faces an inhuman and ghoulish air. This was intensified by the fact that one of them was holding aloft a lance upon which was stuck Eli's bleeding, black-haired head, which appeared to stare sightlessly down at his former comrades.

The men were so taken aback that they did not fire at the two warriors but just stood and stared as the lance was brandished as if in victory, its blood-dripping head waved on high. Whose turn, the men seemed to wonder, would it be next?

'Watch out,' Jock shouted. 'Here come more of them.'

Over the brow of a mountain ridge

was coming a swarm of Hapulchai warriors, running down, leaping from rock to rock, small, fierce-looking men, painted with clay, lances and bows strung with arrows in their hands.

'Get the horses back into the shaft,' Jack roared, grabbing hold of one himself. 'We don't wanna lose the gold.'

His *compadres* saw the sense in this and hurriedly dragged the startled mustangs behind the big rock and into the spacious entrance of the mine shaft.

'Right, men. Get your carbines,' Thad shouted. 'Fire at will.'

They ran out to take up positions behind the big rock but Squat was too eager, facing the oncoming horde with his Winchester in his hands. The carbine appeared to have jammed. A screaming warrior was making a suicidal rush towards him. He hurled his lance. It thudded into the ramrodder's chest and came out of his back, knocking him to the floor. Squat writhed in his death agonies as the warrior raced to finish him with a knife.

Lynch shot the Hapulchai in the side. The Indian leapt like a scalded cat and lay still a few feet from them.

'Jesus!' The sergeant made a mental count. 'That's the fourth of us the mine's claimed. How many more of us are going to die?'

'Unless you put that Henry into action, man,' Lynch shouted, 'you'll be one of them.'

He himself was rapidly firing his Spencer, and the 'firesticks' of the others, their fusillade of lead had told on the Hapulchai. Several of them dropped to their knees and rolled down the slope, like potted jack rabbits, to lie motionless. They were having second thoughts about the wisdom of this headlong rush, and were taking evasive action, dodging behind boulders, but raining arrows down on the intruders.

'We can't hold out here,' Jock McGhee shouted, as he ducked down from the path of the deadly arrows. 'There's too many of them.'

211

Lynch also realized that the odds of about eighty warriors bent on slaughter against five men were not good, even if they had superior arms.

'Back into the shaft, boys. I've had an idea. Try to hold them off at the entrance. I'll be as quick as I can. Come with me, Chollo.'

'What's he think he's up to?' Sergeant Jack asked McGhee as they knelt at the entrance alongside Lonesome and fired their revolvers at the crowd of Indians outside.

'Don't ask me,' Jock cried. 'I doubt if any of us'll live to tell the tale. This place is truly cursed.'

The Sergeant felt a jab in his back and turned to see the conquistador, his sword raised, standing over him.

'What the devil?'

If Jack was surprised, the Hapulchai were more so when they saw what they took to be a Spaniard in armour strut slowly out from the mine, his sword held high. Alongside him was Chollo leading their white-haired priest.

The warriors ceased firing their bows, brandishing their lances, their look of implacable fury changing to astonishment as they stared at the 'God Conquistador' who had come from his cave of shining rock. They began talking and gesticulating fiercely among themselves, and then, almost as one, gave a gasping sigh as Chollo slit the old shaman's throat, holding him upright as the blood and life ebbed from him.

'What did he do that for?' Lonesome asked.

'The Apaches and this tribe have been deadly enemies for years,' Jock said, as awed as the others by the captain's bold stance. 'Look at their faces. I think his bluff's gonna work.'

'Fer Chris'sakes, let's start gittin' these hosses and their loads back outa here and make a run for it while they're in a cowed mood,' Jack roared. 'There was me thinking these painted savages from hell was goin' to carve us up as their next meal.'

Although the Hapulchais were obviously unwilling to attack the imposing figure of Captain Lynch in his armour, would they make the same concessions to the hated Apache and the three other white men who were tentatively edging their heavily loaded pack-horses out of the mine? Or would they slaughter them?

That prickly question would go unanswered, due to an unexpected freak of nature. Suddenly, as the Hapulchais stared threateningly at them, the sky darkened, vivid purple clouds billowing up from behind the Mountain of the Holy Cross. Rapid daggers of lightning streaked across the horizon, flashing in the men's eyes, making them flinch, and the wind became a hot tingling blast against their faces. Even worse, the earth beneath their feet began to vibrate and it was as if the mountain itself trembled. At such moments there are no brave men any more. All who have been in an earthquake will admit to the sheer terror it instils. All around them the mountain range appeared to be dancing, the land quivering and, yes, quaking.

The spur of pines and rock above the mineshaft was no exception. As a spear of lightning daggered down, the Lost Mine caved in upon itself. The men, both white and Indian, screamed and tried to escape as the great rocks of the mountain rearranged themselves, many bouncing pell-mell towards them. All they could do was to run for open land and fling themselves behind other boulders in the hope that they would protect them.

This mammoth earthquake, which is recorded in the history books, did not last long, but in a short space of time totally rearranged the landscape. At last it seemed that it was over. They got to their feet, peering through the yellow haze of dust.

Perhaps the captain had been the best dressed to withstand the blitz of rocks, many of which had bounced off his helmet and breastplate. But many of the Hapulchais had not been so lucky and had been crushed to death or buried alive in the debris. The small company, Lonesome, Sergeant Jack, Jock and Chollo, had somehow survived and went to regroup themselves around Captain Lynch.

He stood bulky and strangely valiant-looking in his armour, still holding his ancient sword, and when the survivors among the Hapulchais saw the 'Spanish Conqueror' their people had worshipped for so long, they fell down on their knees and cried out an ululation of obeisance. Surely, if he had come back to life and had brought this terrible tempest and tremor, he must be the great God Conqueror? He had control of the earth and the skies.

In this part of the North American continent, the short rainy season comes in the summer. And suddenly it was upon them, the virulent black clouds opening. They were in the midst of a downpour now, rain as only rain knows how to fall in Arizona. They looked at the kneeling Hapulchais and laughed loud together. They were gods. For those moments they really felt as if they were. They were free to go and to take what gold they had with them. The Hapulchais were not going to try to stop the Great Conqueror and his motley assistants from leaving.

Captain Lynch in his armour turned to where the mine had been only to find that it had collapsed in on itself and had been sealed off by a wall of rocks. He scratched with his sword a pictogram on the rock of a conquistador's helmet to indicate where the mine had been.

'One day,' he shouted, 'we will return and blast our way into here.'

While his men went to retrieve the terrified horses, none of whom, by a stroke of luck, was badly injured, and their loads still intact, the Hapulchais stayed on their knees praying and chanting.

'It's crazy,' Lynch muttered. 'They really believe I am a god.' He found a sack of tobacco, a tin of sugar, flour, pinto beans and more of their unused stores, which he would have abandoned anyway, and offered them with a gesture of largesse. Then, unhurriedly, but with Sergeant Jack's help, he hoisted himself up on his big dun, raised his hand in stately manner to the crouching Hapulchais, and led his depleted troop down the mountainside. The Indians, once so threatening, merely knelt and watched the last conquistador leave their land.

Ravens were pecking efficiently at the remains of Sam Zabriskie, and strutted a few feet away as they passed.

'Thass what you git fer your double-crossing,' Jack said, and spat.

When they reached the narrow defile of the Black Canyon, where once there had been a trickle of water, they could see from the dampness of its basalt walls that the rainburst must have sent a torrent of water some twelve feet high flooding through. Any horseman caught in it would be swept to his death. And that, they discovered later, was what had happened to Pedro Martinez. His body was only identifiable by his gold teeth. Further on the horse and mule were washed up, their teeth bared in grimaces of agony. Man and beast had been smashed to pulp by the wall of water. They found the torn panniers, but of the quartz there was no sign. It had been scattered back into the wild.

'Pedro's number six,' Sergeant Jack intoned. 'There's just us five left now.'

'Let's hope he's the last,' Lynch snapped, but the way the men looked at each other they all knew that might not be so.

They had camped out overnight in the canyon, but were ready to leave at first light, glancing up apprehensively at the sinister black basalt walls. They might have been overjoyed to have survived the Hapulchais and the earthquake but each man knew they

still had Black Wolf and his *bandidos*
to face.

'Come on, lads,' the captain shouted.
'Get these horses moving. We've a long
way to go.'

13

The towering black-rock cliffs lent the canyon an eerie, threatening air, which threat was fulfilled when a bullet spanged into the dust before the dun's hoofs, making him snort and prance with alarm. The captain, for his own reasons, was still adorned in Spanish armour, and it was as well he was for almost simultaneously another bullet rattled off his helmet. As fast as the armour allowed he climbed from the startled horse and pulled him and his pack-horse into the shadow of some rocks. The others were not slow to follow him as lead whined and ricocheted around them.

'We're trapped,' Sergeant Jack bellowed. 'They're up there on both sides.'

He gave a foul curse as a bullet ripped a line of blood across his temple.

He huddled down, steadied the big old Henry rifle on a rock and sent lead back at their assailants.

The men below looked up and saw a line of horsemen, the mixed gang of Mexicans and Westerners who rode with Black Wolf, silhouetted against the blood-red sky as the blaze of sun fell away behind the cliffs. They had rifles and revolvers in their hands, firing down at them.

One of the Mexicans was pitched from the saddle, and tumbled with a frenzied scream over the cliff.

'He's mine,' Lonesome shouted with jubilation. 'There's one won't be doing no more shooting.'

'No he wasn't, ya crablouse,' Sergeant Jack roared. 'I got him.'

'What does it matter whose he was?' Captain Lynch gritted out as bullets poured from both sides of the canyon. 'They've got us pinned down and that's a fact.'

Chollo crouched beside him, his carbine in his hands, his face grimly set, as if he sensed there was no way they could get out of this. It was just a matter of time before they were all sent spinning into eternity.

'It looks like *el Lobo Negro*'s enrolled some more frontier scum to do his killing,' Jock muttered. 'I've counted twenty, at least. Maybe if we wait for darkness we can make a run for it.'

'I wouldn't count on it, Jock.'

The horsemen had dismounted and were jumping down the rugged cliffs where ways could be found.

'They're closing in on us. Sorry it has to end this way, boys.'

'It ain't ended yet.' The sergeant levered the Henry and dislodged another desperado from his perch. The cliffs echoed to the rattle of gunfire as the trapped men put up a valiant resistance and the bandits tried to cut them to pieces.

'Anyhow,' Jack roared above the explosions, 'it's the way I wanna go — in a blaze of glory.' He grinned through his black beard at them as if in his element in battle. 'Give 'em hell, boys.'

Gradually the shooting slowed into a stalemate, but the trapped men knew by the empty shell-cases scattered around them that it would not be long before their ammunition ran out.

'Hey, look who it ain't,' Jack shouted, raising his smoking rifle. 'Black Wolf.'

The tall figure, his long hair flowing from beneath his tall black hat, was heading towards them with his easy-riding grace, along the floor of the canyon, with two riders in Stetsons and long macinaws on either side of him.

'It's those two *hombres* who had their eyes on us in Tucson,' the captain muttered. 'I was wondering when those jackals would turn up.'

'He's got his white flag,' Lonesome said, as the three horsemen splashed towards them through the canyon stream.

Soon the half-breed was close enough for them to see his gleaming lone eye, his half-handsome, half-scarred face beneath the shadow of his hat.

'It's a trick,' Jock shouted. 'The sneaking curs will kill us all soon as we put our guns aside.'

'It's our only chance,' Captain Lynch replied. 'Hold your fire.'

Black Wolf cantered towards them, white shirt hanging from the barrel of his upraised rifle. About thirty paces away he reined in his mustang and gave his crafty wolflike grin. The two hired guns, one thin-faced and furtive as a ferret, the other clean-shaven but sour of countenance, took their place beside him.

'Don't come no closer,' Jock called, 'or ye'll regret it. What's the deal?'

'Who the hell's *he* in the fancy armour?' the thin-faced *hombre* jeered. 'What's he think this is, a carnival?'

'Who the hell you think I am?' Lynch replied. 'I'm the leader of this bunch and I'm telling you to call off your dogs and go your way. Or else.'

'Or else what? Come on, Captain,' Black Wolf drawled. 'You know we can kill you all if we want to. But I never like bloodshed. Just hand over those horses and their loads and we will spare your lives.'

Lynch's flint-grey eyes peered from beneath the peak of his helmet as he clutched his Spencer in one hand.

'There'll be no surrender by us.'

Black Wolf flashed his bloodthirsty grin again. 'Well, if it ain't my old pal Sergeant Jack. How about you? You've played your cards well. How much gold you got there?'

'Plenty.'

'Plenty for you and us three?' Black Wolf asked. 'You're one of us, Jack. We'll split fair, let bygones be bygones. OK, Jack?'

'Sure, why not?' The burly ex-Confederate stepped forward and turned to stand alongside the three gunmen. 'Too bad, Cap. Never trust an old guerilla fighter. Once a Johnny Reb, always a Johnny Reb.'

'You — I might have guessed, you black-hearted villain. I should have had you strung up.'

'Yeah,' Jack growled, 'an' that's what you were goin' to do when we got back to Tucson, hand me over to the authorities. One less for the share-out.'

'That's not true and you know it. We shook on it. My word's my bond.'

Jack grinned through his beard and gave him a broad wink. 'Too bad mine ain't.'

'I always knew you had a yeller streak down your back, you bag of shit,' Lonesome called. 'You too Black Wolf. Why don't we settle this between us? You four against us four. From a standing draw. Or ain't you got the guts?'

His words rang out clearly in the enclosed canyon, bouncing off the walls and repeating themselves.

'What's the matter, Black Wolf? Ain't you got the guts?'

The *bandidos* had taken advantage of the lull in firing to clamber down the cliff. They stood on rocks and grinned at each other. There was no way Black

Wolf could overlook this insult. Or could he?

'Aye, ye murderin' rapists, ye're all cowards under the skin,' Jock shouted. 'Speak up, mon. Are ye yellow, or not?'

This was not how Black Wolf had planned things, but there was no way he could wriggle out of the challenge. He licked his lips and whispered, 'How about it, boys?'

The cleanshaven *hombre* shrugged, and pulled his macinaw back to reveal the butt of the sixgun slung ready-cocked in a greased holster on his right thigh.

'These scallywags don't bother me.'

'If that's what they want,' the ferret-faced one sneered, 'let's make mincemeat of 'em.' They nodded to each other and dismounted.

'Yeah,' Jack grinned his blackened teeth. 'We'll show 'em how to shoot, shall we, boys?' He tossed his Henry away, moved to one side and took his stance, his good hand patting the long-barrelled revolver stuck in his belt. 'Thirty paces it is.'

The captain removed his helmet and tossed it on to the sand. He unbuttoned the holster on his hip, eased the Colt Navy free, then raised his right hand in readiness, fingers outstretched. 'Let's go for it.'

Chollo put his carbine down, and released his own army-issue holster. It was not built for a fast draw, but his dark eyes were steady as he took his stance beside the captain.

Lonesome took the left flank, his hands hovering over his twin .44s.

'One of you men up there call.'

'I'm ready,' Jock, too, had his revolver stuck in the belt of his tartan trousers. He tugged his tam o'shanter over one eye. 'Prepare to die.'

'*Sí*,' one of *the Mexicans shrilled.* '*Now!*'

The ferret-faced *hombre's* gun came out before the shout, his bullet crashing into the captain's breast-plate, hurling him to the floor.

His companion of the sour countenance had his revolver out too, his slug gunning Jock McGhee down before he could pull his .45 free of his belt.

The Smith & Wessons of Lonesome Jones were out like greased lightning and blazing in his fists. Black Wolf was hit in the arm but, crouching to one side, his sidearm roared to send Chollo spinning in his tracks.

The thin-faced gunman tried to finish the captain with a headshot. Sergeant Jack turned on him, his revolver barking out, blasting the man off his feet.

Black Wolf gave a snarl of surprise and aimed at Jack. But Lonesome's third bullet caught him in the side and he slumped to his knees, gasping 'Agh!'

'Watch out!' Jack shouted as the clean-shaven thug turned his gun on Lonesome, his bullet creasing the youth's neck. Jack raised his heavy Remington and his slug ploughed into the gunman's chest, sending him backtracking to sprawl on his back. The man's expression changed to one of hurt surprise as he stared at the blood pouring from him and slowly succumbed.

All this happened in seconds and suddenly there were five men dead. As the explosions reverberated away along the cliffsides and the sulphurous gunsmoke cleared, Sergeant Jack grinned at the captain and Lonesome.

'You didn't think I'd desert you, did you, boys?'

'Thanks, Sergeant. I must admit I did.' Lynch got to his feet and went to kneel by Jock who was fast suspiring his last. 'I'm sorry I got you into this, old friend.'

'Och, I wouldna have it any other way, Captain. Time has come to let go my weary ghost.' Jock coughed blood and fell back.

The captain confirmed that Chollo too, was dead. He closed the scout's eyes.

'Let your spirit ride free, Chollo. You were a brave man.'

Sergeant Jack kicked at Black Wolf as he lay prone.

'Just making sure he ain't foolin us, the lousy 'breed. Never thought to see him dead before me. As for them other two, well, they were all mouth. They would have killed me in my sleep.'

Lonesome Jones spun his revolvers in his hands, and looked up at the grinning *viciosos* who stood around like a circle of wolves up in the rocks.

'Your leaders are dead. We won,' he called out. 'You gutter trash can clear out. That was the deal.'

'You weesh!' A dark Mexican raised his rifle and fired at him. 'We wan' that gold.'

Jones dodged aside as the bullet took his hat off. He rolled for cover as the bandits sent a hail of bullets their way. The captain dived behind a rock. Jack backed away to crouch beside him.

'The dirty lowdown polecats,' he shouted, and raised his Remington to return fire. 'We're cut off from our rifles. I'm fast running out of ammo, Cap.'

'Yes.' Lynch took aim at their assailants. 'It looks like none of us are going to get out of this.'

'Yeah,' Jack grunted. 'All that digging so these bastards can benefit.'

'What do you mean, man? You didn't do any digging.' Lynch grinned side-long at him, and held his fire. 'Wait a minute. Look who's up there. It's not over yet.'

'Damn me,' Jack yelled. 'It's the Hapulchais.' He hooted with glee as the warriors hurled lances and fired arrows into the backs of the surprised *viciosos*, leaping down to finish them with their knives. 'Jeesus! I never thought I'd be rescued by a band of bloodthirsty redskins.'

14

They were indeed rescued. Black Wolf's 'frontier scum', caught between two lines of fire, were massacred to a man. Captain Lynch replaced his helmet and found his sword to raise aloft, welcoming the Hapulchais, who gathered around him, less servile now, revealing themselves as the warlike savages they were.

'I guess we oughta get outa here,' the captain said, as darkness fell. 'There's a full moon fit to rise, a clear sky. It'll be as bright as daylight.'

The warriors had lit a fire and were roasting a haunch of one of the horses that had been killed in the gunfight. The captain kept the mounts of Black Wolf and his two sidekicks and indicated to the Hapulchais that the *bandidos'* mustangs at the top of the cliffs were theirs. He also presented them with a couple of rocks of quartz.

'They seem to know how to smelt it down,' he said. 'Better sweeten 'em with something.'

They organized their pack- and saddle-horses and bade farewell once more to the feasting, yelling warriors. They moved away into the darkness.

'Strikes me it's more'n pony they're chewin' on,' Sergeant Jack chuckled. 'Poor departed Black Wolf an' his sidekicks didn't realize their livers would be savages' suppers tonight.'

★ ★ ★

It was a long, hard journey back, and they didn't breathe easy until they were down through the oak forest and reaching the foothills. Thaddeus Lynch had removed his armour, carefully packing it on one of the spare horses.

'It's amazing how well-preserved it is,' he mused. 'Hardly a speck of rust. Must be from being in that dry cool air of the mine. But it's hellish hot to wear. Don't know how those Spaniards bore it in these temperatures.'

'It was either that or get an arrow in their chest,' Lonesome replied. 'It saved you a couple of times, Cap.'

'Yes, it did. Perhaps the ghost's changed his mind about putting a curse on me. When I die I'll leave him to the museum.'

They were back on the lowland stretch, riding through cactus and rocks, and he turned in the saddle to look back at the dark and mysterious range of the Superstition mountains. 'Well, it's unveiled its secret at last.'

'Will you be going back, Cap? There's all that gold still there.'

'No, I don't think so. Let the mountain keep its gold. We've got enough for our needs. If not more.'

'When you think about it,' Lonesome said, 'in the past six weeks, if you count Don Pico's party, all Black Wolf's boys, the Hapulchais, and our own men gone, there's about forty people died on account of this gold.'

'Gold does strange things to men, Lonesome.'

'What are *you* going to do with your share, Cap? Gonna retire back east and live the life of O'Reilly?'

'I do have relatives back there. No, I've lived on the frontier for thirty years now. Arizona Territory's my home. I believe Grace feels the same,' he murmured. 'Her family made the trek out here and they've fought for the right to stay.'

'Hear tell some drunken rascal called Geronimo, a nephew of Cochise, has been stirring up trouble,' Sergeant Jack put in. 'Arizona could be a war zone again.'

'We've taken the Apache terror before, we'll take it some more,' Lynch gritted out. 'I have sympathy with their problems. They've been treated badly. But they can never defeat us. This is our land now.'

'Yep,' Jack laughed. 'Poor ol' Injins. They allus git a raw deal. But I sure am feelin' kindlier towards 'em since meetin' them Hapulchais.'

★ ★ ★

If the captain had still been wearing the suit of armour he couldn't have created more of a stir as they trailed their tired horses back into Tucson. When they approached the old adobe walls and rumour of their arrival spread through the settlement, the first to greet them was Marie, running out barefoot in her loose blouse and crimson skirt, towards them.

'I'll see ya, Cap,' Lonesome shouted. 'You can send me my share.' He spurred his shaggy paint forward and as he reached the girl, scooped her up and swung her behind his saddle. He raised an arm in farewell and galloped on into the township.

'He's in one helluva hurry,' Jack said.

'They're young and in love.' The captain smiled. 'Come on. I'm gonna get this quartz assayed and lodged in the bank. Then its the bathhouse and a good meal with my knees under a table for a change. You with me?'

When they had put back a repast of enchiladas and tortillas in the Shoofly restaurant, so named for all the flies they had to shoo off their food, the captain sat back and said, 'We're wealthy men, Jack. What will you do? Go back to Missouri? Kill yourself with whiskey?'

'Four weeks without it. I ain't nevuh felt so fit, Cap. I'm gonna take it easy on the juice, give my liver a chance. I wanna enjoy life. Nah, I'm staying in Arizona, too.' He picked at his teeth with a fingernail, and grinned through his beard. 'I'm plannin' on making ol' Rosetta a honest woman. We gonna git wed.'

The captain pulled the cork of a bottle of best Irish whiskey. 'A special treat.' He poured it into their tumblers. 'Two jolts apiece might just about cut the dust.'

Sergeant Jack winked at him and

raised his glass. The bottle didn't last long but imparted a warm glow. Jack got to his feet.

'You thinkin' what I'm thinkin'? We could make it back to the Welcome Stranger tonight. We got fresh hosses outside.'

Lynch stood and paid the bill.

'Exactly my thoughts.'

They ran outside, jumped on their mounts and set off hell for leather across the sage and mesquite.

'Yee-hagh!' Jack yelled. 'Let's go see them purty gals.'

* * *

It was a long ride and dawn was flushing the sky pink and gold by the time they sighted the adobe waystation. Jack's rebel yell roused Rosetta who was out at the well, and she was joined by Grace and young Ben. The riders hauled in in a cloud of dust and Thad Lynch stared at the young woman, who was holding a baby in her arms.

'Who's that?' he asked.

'She's ours.' Grace smiled anxiously. 'She's the daughter of Doña Esmeralda. They were going to send her back East to an orphanage. Can we keep her, Thad?'

'We sure can.' The captain jumped down and hugged the three of them. 'We can afford a big family now.'

Sergeant Jack whooped and scooped up Rosetta, whirling her around. He wiggled the forefinger of his good hand at the baby and, as she clutched at it, a smile creased his face.

'I can be her grandaddy. Only' — he paused in afterthought — 'we better not tell her what happened to her mama. At least, not 'til I'm dead and gawn.'

Author's Note

This fiction is based on fact. More than forty men are reported to have perished searching for the Lost Mine of the Superstitions.

We do hope that you have enjoyed reading this large print book.

Did you know that all of our titles are available for purchase?

We publish a wide range of high quality large print books including:
Romances, Mysteries, Classics
General Fiction
Non Fiction and Westerns

Special interest titles available in large print are:
The Little Oxford Dictionary
Music Book, Song Book
Hymn Book, Service Book

Also available from us courtesy of Oxford University Press:
Young Readers' Dictionary
(large print edition)
Young Readers' Thesaurus
(large print edition)

For further information or a free brochure, please contact us at:
Ulverscroft Large Print Books Ltd.,
The Green, Bradgate Road, Anstey,
Leicester, LE7 7FU, England.
Tel: (00 44) **0116 236 4325**
Fax: (00 44) **0116 234 0205**

The stage robbery had been accomplished by an old woman. Twine Fourch had never heard of a female being a highway robber before. He followed the trail all the way to a dilapidated log cabin up Stone Mountain. What happened after that no one could believe even after townsmen from Jefferson found the old log house and the skeletal dying old woman. But before the mystery could be solved there would be two unnecessary killings, a bizarre suicide and a lynching.

GUNS OF THE GAMBLER

M. Duggan

Destitute gambler Ben Crow arrives in Mallory keen to claim his inheritance, only to discover that rancher Edward Bacon has other ideas. Set up by Miss Dorothy, who had fooled him completely, Ben finds himself dangling on the end of a rope. Saved from death, Ben sets off in pursuit of Miss Dorothy, determined upon retribution. However, his quest for vengeance turns into a rescue mission when she is kidnapped by a crazy man-burning bandit.

SIDEWINDER

John Dyson

All Flynn wants is to be Marshal of Tucson, but he is framed by the territory's richest rancher, Frank Buchanan, and thrown into Yuma prison. Five years later Flynn comes out, intent on clearing his name and burning for vengeance. Fists thud, knives flash and bullets fly as he rides both sides of the law and participates in kidnapping and double-dealing. He is once again arrested for a murder of which he is innocent. Can he escape the noose a second time?

THE BLOODING OF JETHRO

Frank Fields

When Jethro Smith's family is murdered by outlaws, vengeance is the one thing on his mind. He meets the brother of one of the murderers, who attempts to exploit Jethro's grudge in the pursuit of his own vendetta. The local preacher, formerly a sheriff, teaches Jethro how to use a gun. With his new-found skills, Jethro and his somewhat unwelcome friend pit themselves against seemingly impossible odds. Whatever the outcome lead would surely fly.